Emma Lathen

An Elizabeth Thatcher Mystery

dot.com murder

"Thatcher is Nero Wolfe with portfolio"

"The American Agatha Christie"

New York Times Book Reviews

Simply Media Inc.
POB 481
Lincoln, MA 01773-0481
www.simplymedia.com

24 John Putnam Thatcher
Emma Lathen Mysteries

1. Banking on Death 1961. Manufacturing basics.
2. A Place for Murder 1963. Old Rich v Towns People.
3. Accounting for Murder 1964. Accounting.
4. Murder Makes the Wheels Go Round 1966. Cars.
5. Death Shall Overcome 1966. Integration.
6. Murder Against the Grain 1967. Options Trading.
7. A Stitch in Time 1968. Health Care.
8. Come to Dust 1968. Fund Raising.
9. When in Greece 1969. International Business.
10. Murder to Go 1969. Fast Food.
11. Pick Up Sticks 1970. Second Home Developments.
12. Ashes to Ashes 1971. Real Estate Development.
13. The Longer the Thread 1971. Cut & Sew Off Shore
14. Murder Without Icing 1972. Professional Sports.
15. Sweet and Low 1974. Candy Bars & Consumer.
16. By Hook or by Crook 1975. Antique Rugs.
17. Double, Double, Oil and Trouble 1978. Oil.
18. Going for the Gold 1981. Olympics/Amateur Sport.
19. Green Grow the Dollars 1982. Mail Order/Nursery.
20. Something in the Air 1988. Discount Airlines.
21. East is East 1991. International, Robotics & Finance.
22. Right on the Money 1993. Mergers & Acquisitions.
23. Brewing Up a Storm 1996. Beer.
24. A Shark Out of Water 1997. Government Projects.

6 Elizabeth & John Putnam Thatcher

Emma Lathen Mysteries

John Putnam Thatcher reorganizes the Sloan, becomes Chairman, Charlie Trinkham President, Ken Nicholls SVP, Elizabeth Thatcher Head of IT & Venture Capital, Walter Bowman VP of Yes, Everett Gabbler VP of No & Maria Corsa, Miss Corsa's niece, a direct report to Elizabeth Thatcher. George Lancer, former Chairman, Brad Withers, former President & Miss Corsa are retired but curious.

The Sloan has automated its branches, moved Corporate HQ to Ireland, set up IT in India, established the VC division in Ireland & Austin, and sold off the Sloan HQ building in New York. The Sloan has gone private with the above active individuals being the major shareholders and become the largest Bank in the World by Capital value.

25. **Political Murder** 1999. Death of a Senator.
26. **Dot Com Murder** 2001. Death of a Dot Com Leader.
27. **Biking Murder** 2005. Death of a Bike Lane Advocate.
28. **Nonprofit Murder** 2008. Death of a Nonprofit CEO.
29. **Union Murder** 2010. Death of a Union Leader.
30. **Gig Murder**. 2016. Death of a Gig Innovator.

dot.com murder
contents

preface

Henissart and Latsis attended Harvard graduate school back in the day. They discovered they were running out of traditional mysteries to read such as Agatha Christie and Rex Stout. They also learned that most mystery buffs had similar experiences leading to the eternal question: What's next?

At first they were friends and then roommates. Latsis worked in the CIA and spent two years in Rome employed by the UN's Food and Agricultural Organization before returning to Wellesley College to teach Economics. Henissart went to New York to practice law.

In 1960 Henissart took a corporate legal job at Raytheon in Boston and stayed with Latsis during her house hunt. She asked what good mysteries were around and was told there weren't any left.

They then said, "Let's write one." With that they were off and running in their lifetime entrepreneurial writing venture. This reminded me of my old friend Alex Goodwin, now Levitch, the only man I know who has ever changed his last name not to his wife's, bringing me the Umbroller type stroller as a business project and I said, "Let's do it." We did. We were Choate roommates and had gone our separate ways until we had our first taste of organization life for me at General Foods and Alex in law at the US Justice Dept. in DC.

Latsis and Henissart had an unusual relationship for writers but not for entrepreneurial partners. They began each work by first agreeing on the basic structure and major characters; then they wrote alternating chapters. Latsis then composed the first complete draft on yellow pads and produced this edition for Henissart to review. Henissart then typed out the final draft.

They would then get together for a final joint rewrite, eliminating inconsistencies, and synthesizing the work into a coherent whole. Unlike the tradition of a Hemingway and Fitzgerald with an editor like Max Perkins, they jointly did their own editor work as equal partners in their enterprise.

Most mystery buffs have had that moment of running out of acceptable books to read. Each of us can remember vividly the wonderful moment when we found another series to read. This can be your moment with the Emma Lathen series!

I can remember the moment I learned about Sue Grafton, Thomas Perry, Dick Francis, and Emma Lathen herself. Some tap out and get off track like Patricia Cornwell, but they are often terrific while on track.

Being practical as well as talented people, Henissart and Latsis took up the challenge and wrote 31 books together before Latsis died in 1997.

24 were Emma Lathen John Thatcher books and 7 Ben Stafford political works written under the name R. G. Dominic. As good entrepreneurs, they let the Stafford series go when the John Thatcher series outsold it by a substantial amount.

The series has been extended to six more featuring Thatcher's daughter, Elizabeth, and most of the rest of the cast, this time moving Thatcher up to Chairman, Trinkam President, Nicholls SVP, Elizabeth Head of IT & VC, Bowman VP of Yes, Gabbler VP of No, and Miss Corse's niece on board working for Elizabeth. Lancer, Withers, and Rose Corsa have retired but remain shareholders and are curious as well.

There will be more as The Sloan adapts to the modern world by having moved their HQ to Ireland in a tax inversion, automating its branches to be more mobile and less subject to regulation, centering IT in India, venture capital in Austin, going private, and becoming the largest bank in the world measured by capital value.

Henissart studied law at Harvard after graduating in physics from Mt. Holyoke. Latsis studied economics at Wellesley and

Harvard so setting their books in the business world suited both of them. Their seemingly infallible instincts helped them recognize that business people were big mystery readers and could afford to buy a series, exactly what my Aunt Dorothy did.

Martha Henissart chuckled when telling me their best book store was on Wall Street itself.

They created the name Emma Lathen out of a combination of letters in their own names, something they had great fun doing. M of Mary and Ma of Martha, and Lat of Latsis and Hen of Henissart. This was reinforced by Emma from Jane Austen. And viola--Emma Lathen was born!

No one troubled to find out who Emma Lathen was for years. The authors kept it quiet to protect Henissart's clients from possible embarrassment.

They created an ensemble of characters to enrich their stories and carry people's knowledge about the Thatcher group from book to book, much like Agatha did to a more limited extent with Hastings and Jap joining Poirot in many books. Emma Lathen anticipated TV series such as Mary Tyler Moore and later Friends that created a cast of characters so we knew them from the beginning of a story and didn't have to labor to learn a new group.

Pure   whipped   cream   without   the   calories.

introduction

Emma Lathen used Wall Street, banking, and business as the backdrop for her inspiration for a series of entertaining mysteries. The New York Times said, "John Putnam Thatcher is Nero Wolfe with portfolio." In fact many readers turn to Lathen when they have finished the Nero Wolfe stories. Another New York Times reviewer said, "Emma Lathen is the American Agatha Christie."

An LA review from the Daily News said, "The Agatha Christie of Wall Street."

With those accolades she surely deserves our respect. More personally, she is worthy of reading, especially after you have run out of Wolfe and Christie mysteries.

What is most charming about this 24 book series is that her entourage is in all the books, much like successful TV series such as Friends. Rex Stout had a similar group but they didn't appear in every mystery. Agatha Christie had Captain Hastings, Miss Lemon, and Japp who appeared together occasionally; the TV series got them into more episodes to the delight of Agatha fans.

I was personally introduced to Lathen by my Aunt Dorothy who was a business woman back in the day building houses in Minneapolis and then in World War II moving on to Seattle with her husband to do so. Interestingly, this is the only author my Aunt ever recommended. I have been forever grateful to her for doing so. Much like a Lathen character, my Aunt knew what money was good for and what it wasn't. Uncle Chester and she built houses in the warm six months in Minneapolis and later Seattle, and then took off the other six to enjoy worldwide cruises for the rest of the year.

Her postcards let me follow her from country to country, place to place, as they had a grand old time of it. She was introduced to Lathen in a ship's library with the books bound in lovely yellow sturdy boards produced by Lathen's English publisher. It all seemed to fit; English like Christie; on ship; with business people who could relate to Lathen and her cast of characters.

Emma Lathen was the pseudonym for Martha Henissart and Mary Jane Latsis who wrote 24 adeptly structured detective stories featuring a banker, John Putnam Thatcher, and crack amateur sleuth much like Jane Marple. Thatcher is every bit as endearing and interesting as Poirot and Marple, Nero Wolfe and Archie, and Sue Grafton's Kinsey Millhone, Henry, and company.

Each story starts out with a business/banking motif, points to motives other than money, and winds up with money not emotions being the clue to the solution. Thatcher's clear headed knowledge of money, banking, business, and human foibles is as only bankers can know, leads to his eureka moments, which are always fabulously turned out.

Thatcher's purpose is curiosity coupled with a desire to get his loans and the bank's investments repaid which leads to his delivering killers to the police, signed, sealed, and delivered.

Why was banking as a back drop for these mysteries? Henissart and Latsis put it best, "There is nothing on God's earth a banker can't get into." Voila, and much like their rapier like insights and wits of these charming tough minded authors.

Thatcher was the first fictional detective to come out of the world of business and finance. He became an instant hit on Wall Street and beyond in business and financial circles. This makes him perfect for today's millennial and Z generations so enthusiastic about entrepreneurial life in education, nonprofits, and commercial life, all of which are represented in the work of Emma   Lathen.

cast

Regulars

John Putnam Thatcher, SVP of the Sloan, the Third Largest Bank in the World.

Charlie Trinkam, Thatcher's Second in Command in the Trust Department.

Everett Gabbler, the informal VP of No, who identifies the weaknesses in every situation.

Walter Bowman, the informal VP of Yes, who advocates new investment opportunities.

Ken Nicholls, the budding young banker, recently married, with his second child on the way.

Miss Rose Corsa, the irrepressible old time tough secretary to top executives as she is to Thatcher.

Tom Robichaux, Investment Banker/promoter, much married, a bon vivant, with conservative proper Quaker Devane as his partner. Thatcher's Harvard Roommate back in the day.

George Charles Lancer, Stately Chairman of the Board.

Lucy Lancer, the perceptive witty wife of George.

Elizabeth ("Becky") Thatcher, John Putnam Thatcher's second daughter, stunning, smart, and much like his abolitionist grandmother. VP of IT & VC investments.

Occasional Characters

Professor Cardwell ("Cardy") Carlson, the father-in-law of Laura, Thatcher's daughter. An erudite impractical professor.

Mrs. Agnes Carlson, the mother-in-law that keeps Ben in line and up to form.

Dr. Ben Carlson, Thatcher's son-in-law. Stays quietly in the background.

Laura Thatcher Carlson, Thatcher's first daughter & family organizer.

Jack Thatcher, youngest of the Thatcher children and much like Tom Robichaux and hence now the junior partner in the firm of Robichaux, Devane & Thatcher.

Jane Schneider Nicholls, wife of Ken.

Sam, Sloan Chauffer.

Billings, the sardonic respectful elevator operator.

Don Trotman, the Devonshire Doorman and Jack of all Trades onsite.

Albert Nelson, John Thatcher's man servant and general helper.

Characters only in *Dot Com Murder*

Dave Brown, founder of Simply and serial entrepreneur.

John "Jack" Towson, Dot Com founder & CEO, Evangelist at everything.com.

Janet Brown, next generation leader at Simply who engineered sale to everything.com.

Charles "Chuck" Newberg, COO and Operating leader at everything.com. Pushed the acquisition of Simply for cashflow, profitability, stability, and in a related download niche.

Bruce Dahl, VP Marketing & Sales. Openhanded, creative, underestimated for his uncanny shrewdness. In it for the money.

Jim Johnson, CFO, limited silo thinker but a virtuoso within the silo.

Jackie Marlow, VP Social Media, an open-minded unbiased thinker, generous in spirit and action, savvy corporate politician.

Amar Prince, Data, straightforward, analytical, creative, and a true Internationalist being raised in India, educated in England, and then to MIT for a data analytics PHD. Openhanded, kind, but does not suffer fools or foolish behavior well.

George Parsons, Considered the best New York City Detective. Thick-skinned, subtle, hardboiled, and lots more, as needed.

Joyce Allison, Sargent working for Parsons; private schools, Manhattan native, who wanted to go over to the wild side. Would certainly become Commissioner someday as a Columbia College grad.

Pietro Romano, Rich Italian business owner who dealt with Chuck because he would negotiate versus Jack who would not, despite Jack being more to his taste.

The Man, a rich semi-legitimate business person who had invested in Romano early and Romano owed big time. Dangerous in his own way if crossed; a great friend if supported.

Emma Lathen Political Mysteries

As R. B. Dominic

1.Murder Sunny Side Up 1968. Agriculture.
2.Murder in High Place 1969. Overseas Travelers.
3.There is No Justice 1971. Supreme Court.
4.Epitaph for a Lobbyist 1974. Lobbyists.
5.Murder Out of Commission 1976. Nuke Plants.
6.The Attending Physician 1980. Health Care.
7.Unexpected   Developments   1983.   Military.

Tom Walker Mysteries
Patricia Highsmith

01.18. Football & Superbowl.
02.Abduct. Sexual Misconduct.
03.Body. Planned Eliminations for Money.
04.Comfortable. Avoiding Consequences.
05.Death. Wrong Place at the Wrong Time.
06.Enthusiast. Opportunity Murder.
07.Fraud. Taking Your Chances.
08.Greed. Heirs Who Know Better.
09.Heat. Heir Arrogance.

A similarly popular Simply Media mystery series.

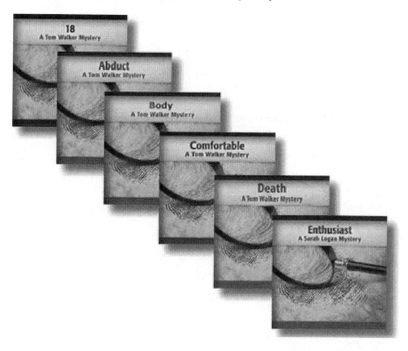

Financial & Other Facts

Emma Lathen is all about the money not the emotion. In that light:

1. Find us at Kindle and elsewhere such as walmart.com, staples.com, amazon.com, barnesandnoble.com (bn.com), and via Overdrive, Findaway, Hoopla, Midwest Tapes, and others. Listen to the audiobook versions at audible.com, iTunes, and elsewhere.

2. To provide financial incentives for collectors, Simply Media and others provide savings on groups of 6 eBooks, and the SuperSku (learning from the Star Wars franchise) "all in" collection.

3. Trust that we have all enjoyed this. But as Willie Nelson, Oscar Wilde, and others have said, we aren't above the money. Stay well. And thanks from all of us on the Emma Lathen team.

Deaver Brown, Publisher.
www.simplymedia.com

Chapter 1

lunch

Wall Street is just like any gossipy country store

Wall Street is the greatest money market in the world. This means, among other things, that it is a quivering communications network, plucking data from cyberspace, speeding it to people who make or lose millions by knowing things before the rest of the world. The first tremor of turmoil in Germany sets off gold dealers on Broad Street to text their branch offices in London, Geneva, or Mumbai. Gossip about a British cabinet minister can trigger frenzied activity on Blair Street. No New York investment bank like Lehman Brothers has failed recently, but Wall Street retains an indelible memory of what happened when one did.

In a word, Wall Street routinely deals with news that does not break into print. Intelligence crucial to the peace of the world, the fortunes of men and women, and the fate of nations is grist to the financial world's mill.

It does not always preclude plain gossip as the subject of Wall Street's conversation.

"What's this about everything.com buying Simply for $2 billion cash? Do they want to mess up that cash machine or will it boost the everything.com stock or both?" asked Jack Thatcher, recently made a name partner at Robichaux, Devane & Thatcher, New York's leading boutique investment bankers.

His lunch partner was Elizabeth Thatcher, Head of the Sloan's Ireland VC & IT division and inline to be the next generation's leader at the Sloan, now the largest bank in the world as well as being private to be more agile, less regulated, and a boon for its few stockholders, the Thatchers being major ones. Elizabeth was also his sister but somehow they kept a Chinese wall between their business and personal life. John Putnam Thatcher, Chairman of the Sloan, and their father, never quite figured out how they did that.

As Wall Street insiders, the Thatchers probably dealt in knowledge more recondite than most. Elizabeth, Becky to her family and Elizabeth in her professional life, agreed that the deal was challenging.

"Brown is a throwback to the days when companies had to earn a profit or at least have some hope of it. He is selling out Simply and evidently won't have a say in everything.com," Jack mused. As the ultimate sales guy, he was optimistic, if unrealistic by nature, and he continued, "Imagine what everything.com could be worth if it was the only dot com that was profitable. He could help do it; but evidently won't be allowed to do so. Our shares would soar; our clients would love us who are still in it; it would be plain great."

"Dream on Jack." Elizabeth said as the realist in business and their family life, like her late mother.

Jack was a bon vivant in the mold of his Senior Partner, Tom Robichaux, his father's old Harvard College roommate, but without Tom's need to have serial wives. Jack had managed to have the fun, or at least most of it, without divorce-court by the simple means of never having married.

With perhaps a more balanced perspective, or perhaps with his generation's more realistic view of human relationships, Jack sighed and said, "Yes, yes, I know. And if pigs could fly, etc. and so on," as he paused.

Elizabeth smiled. One of her pleasures talking with Jack is he could play both sides of the net, batting the ball back and forth, sometimes with the speed of tennis and other times at full tilt like ping pong. She wondered what speed level he would

2

achieve now. Tennis she thought. He confirmed it by slowing down and saying, "And what will the Sloan do with its Simply VC investment?"

"Well we cashed in our everything.com stock as soon as we could legally dispose of it, which took a while. We came out well. Better than lately from what I see with their fluctuating stock prices."

Jack paused over his fruit dessert, quite the opposite of the apple pie a la mode Tom liked and somehow managed to have routinely without gaining any weight, "What about Simply?" getting back to his original question.

"Jack, the simple answer is we will dividend the $100 million out; we have no immediate need of it for investment capital and our few shareholders, including Dad and me, like cold hard cash," as she grinned. "And you too, of course."

"Of course," he said with his endearing smile which closed more than a few accounts, which he knew full well.

Elizabeth went on to say, "The offer was something Brown couldn't really refuse. He runs a tight ship and Janet, the CEO now, is a chip off the old block as well as being tuned into the millennial and z generation behind it. She still has him responsible for carrying the water."

Jack nodded and followed up with a sales guy's question, "I'll betcha he likes that too. What does he talk about? Worry about? And what's he thinking?"

Elizabeth paused to answer. "He says he doesn't understand why dot coms have all the trappings of traditional companies when they don't need them. You know, receptionists, big lobbies, that sort of thing. Of course, I don't know either but that's what he tends to talk about."

Jack nodded her on, so she went on, "We made our $2 million investment in Simply so Walmart would think they could handle more business. Brown said they didn't need the money but needed the Sloan's support to help with Simply's reputation and balance sheet for Walmart. We agreed it was a reasonable proposition, as you may recall, and we did it promptly."

"That worked. Simply repaid us promptly so we only got 5% of the company; if it had taken longer we would have gotten 10%. But, as you know, better to have a going blowing company than one that staggers along; so the 5% was and is fine. It is rather a big deal for us since we treated the investment as a loan due to Simply's prompt repayment with interest. It will be a big cash payout for us at a $2 billion sales price."

"In fact, a wow deal for us since it took little effort to do in the beginning, almost no oversight was required while they had the $2 million, and thereafter it was almost like money in the bank. Of course, we are corporately out of everything.com now so we don't have much risk there except for some of our trust accounts that still hold some despite our advice not to do so."

Jack asked, "How much is that?"

Elizabeth said, "I'm afraid to ask. The Trust department reports separately to Uncle Charlie. They have kept that number quiet. Everything.com is a real mess in my opinion, but you know people think I have a touch too much of Uncle Everett in me." Uncle Everett, Everett Gabbler, was literally the VP of No in the now private Sloan Bank. He had a unique gift for finding the funny bone in anything, a good thing to a point but after that he could drive people crazy, and often did.

Jack ended their lunch by saying, "I didn't need that much truth because some of our clients still have some too, that we haven't been able to talk them into selling. If it goes up in price it is them holding out; if it goes down it is our fault for leaving them in. No way for us to win in this," he lamented.

Elizabeth noted that Jack had picked up Uncle Tom's habit of crying in his beer, but still having plenty of it so to speak. All of Jack's investors had made a bundle with everything.com; Jack had succeeded in making all of them cash in at least half so they were all in the high clover and way ahead on their original investment basis, no matter what happened now.

Jack's laments had always worked for Tom Robichaux to make his clients feel sorry for him, and others as well, so she thought this was a good developing habit of Jack's for Robichaux, Devane & Thatcher.

Chapter 2

simply

The difference between making a buck & losing one is more than 2 bucks

Brown, founder of Simply and serial entrepreneur, was sitting with his daughter, Janet, now CEO, in his townhouse in Lincoln, Massachusetts. It was a lot smaller than the big house they had had on the lake in Lincoln that Brown called his Marriott. Large, spacious, rambling, and fine for his family of 5 kids. But, and it was a big but, he liked a simpler life as a former canoe guide and was a Thoreau groupie, according to him and others. His mantra was Thoreau's, "Simplify simplify."

Many people knew Thoreau's <u>Walden Pond</u> but Brown preferred <u>Walking</u>, a mellow book relating to how Thoreau saw and got everything out of life just traipsing around nearby Concord, now built up. But nearby Lincoln was not so much, so Brown lived there. He liked to say he only lived a mile or two from Walden Pond so as to keep in touch with his soulmate so to speak.

Brown also emphasized that Thoreau was a successful businessman with a pencil factory and railed on against taxes like any Republican of the modern era. Brown himself was a libertarian, but found the party too small to do much with. He was big on the safety net, but not the bureaucratic goings on that cost everyone.

He traveled much like a canoe guide; a small bag with his electronic gear; 1 change of clothes; a toothbrush, razor, and no pills at 72. He walked at least 12,000 steps per day; had stopped any strenuous exercise due to age issues; and was back below his college weight due to less muscle and less stress without 5 kids at home, now having a smaller place, and his wife occupied working.

Janet, on the other hand, enjoyed a more wide ranging middle aged life with husband, 2 children, a nice house on a nearby lake, access to their Brown family house in the New Hampshire White Mountains, and a bedroom devoted to her clothes. However, she was a chip off the old block regarding simplicity and keeping the business that way.

With that background in mind, and their whole life reflected in it, they were considering everything.com's offer to buy Simply for $2 billion cash, an enormous sum in their minds since they owned the company free and clear, and had for a long time, except for the 5% stock owned by the Sloan.

"You know, Janet, everything.com is a ridiculous name but it seems to be very fashionable."

"Yes and the name is tongue in cheek."

"Yes, we must give them that. As you know, Jan, I've always been a pretty good minor league entrepreneur, starting in manufacturing when that's all there was, having 100s of people to manage which seemed impossible at the time and even worse in retrospect. I have no idea how Walmart can run millions; I could barely do 100s back then."

Janet knew this wasn't true. He was legendary among his employees; but it had worn him down. She remembered her mother telling her she didn't mind the sheriffs calling him at night to bail an employee out; but she did mind that he knew them by voice and liked them.

"Jan," she had said. "He posted bail all over town so the tool makers wouldn't have to hock their tools to get bail and lose a day's work. He had a standing rule that anyone jailed like that could come in at noon without having to talk about it at all; ridiculous but effective."

"What did he say about it?" Janet had asked.

"He said they only got drunk and jailed when they get anxious and couldn't wait for hunting season to start. Then they could informally disappear and justify going away from their responsibilities by hunting. Some hunted; some just went away, according to him. It was fine with him; never get into it was his motto. Few people could do it; but few could do what he did either."

"He used to tell me that dealing with tolerances as tool makers must, and having to get everything exactly right, wore them down. Not like engineers who just drafted stuff though he loved his engineers too."

"But he had an engineering background."

"Yes, but that meant he understood. And he had a gift for knowing people; it just wore him down. In his next time he was focused on having fewer employees and did. Then he decided to get into a business with no employees, and that's Simply, just contractors and cyberspace."

"What else?"

"Nothing really; he likes the lack of stress. As a younger man he could deal with it. He likes being old and slow, though he doesn't act old and he isn't slow. He is a good showman of course," and she smiled. She still liked him some while most older wives didn't like their husbands at all, or most men for that matter. She kept her point of view to herself but thought that men ran off by and large not for younger flesh but after happier women. Many of her female friends had had that problem, but she never let on why because then she would have lost them as friends. She sighed. Janet soon nodded. It had been a memorable and therapeutic conversation for both of them.

She was back to her father in her CEO role now. He saw she was back and introduced the subject of their get together.

8

"So we have a $2 billion offer. Our business is as simple and routine now as shooting fish in a barrel. Not much fun or sport in that. Jan, it is up to you. You are in charge now. What do you want to do?"

"This is an inflated offer. We did have $100 million in net profit on only $110 million in sales; we have a simple system selling the lowest priced and high quality audiobooks and eBooks. Our New York competitors, who are the only ones we have, still have old style hierarchical structures that require high pricing. We will continue to get royalties for 90% of the titles we produced ourselves or own outright. So that's another $10 million or so a year. So, let's do it."

Her dad said, "Yeah, reminds me of a great scene in *Heaven Can Wait* with Warren Beaty and Julie Christie as actors at their best when the Beaty character when reincarnated as a billionaire buys the LA Rams. The seller, a great character actor whose face is familiar but not his name, says about selling the team, "He stole it from me." When asked how, he said, "He offered me far more than it was worth so I had to take it."

"Rather like us. But like him, we'll take the money. OK. Let's let them know," and they did then by text as well as faxing over their 1 page signed agreement.

As Brown had said in the past, "Just because there are more zeroes doesn't mean things have to be more complicated. And I got that from Sam Walton back in the day. Great point as were so many of his."

The Agreement called for $1.9 billion to be wired to the Simply Sloan account and $100 million to the Sloan investment account in Ireland. In return, everything.com got 100% ownership of their 100 shares with no contingencies, guarantees, employment contracts, or any other hanging obligations other than to continue paying royalties on their homemade titles if they chose to use them. If not, they returned them to Brown personally. Simple, easy, neat, with no lawyers or advisers involved.

Chapter 3

everything

The salad days never last long enough

Jack Towson and Charles "Chuck" Newberg smiled as they looked at the signed 1 page fax from Simply. They had wisely signed the copy sent to Simply so once they signed it, the deal was done without the complexities of lawyers or advisors involved.

They had bagged the cashflow elephant, though a tiny stock valuation compared to their own heady one of $16 billion.

They had no cash but they had lots of currency in their stock. They believed that on the announcement they would get the company for free just on the stock price boost. They would be right and more.

Chuck had managed to borrow the $2 billion on a short term basis pledging stock to the Sloan to let them liquefy automatically as soon as their stock hit a market cap of $20 billion or whatever the market cap was in a week if it didn't make $20 billion before then.

So with the signed agreement in hand, faxed to the Sloan that handled their money, and the $2 billion loan on the above basis, they drew down on their Sloan loan to wire $1.9 billion to Simply and $100 million to the Sloan VC division. Incestuous; all in the family, Elizabeth chuckled when she heard the money had hit the Sloan account. Essentially an infinite return given the Sloan never had any money out to get the 5% in the first place. The money had been allocated to the first 5%, plus interest, which was repaid in full on time.

With that all done in less than 5 minutes with a receipt from the Sloan, Jack and Chuck shut the door, lit up their non-PC cigars, Chuck swigged some cheap Kirkland Costco bourbon that was fabulous, and enjoyed the moment, while Jack had a fancy brandy suiting his high end tastes. They were long time roommates at Harvard College and Business School. They had continued that tradition when launching everything.com out of their HBS dorm room much like Michael Dell had from his at Texas.

They lived now in two great condos next to each other in a pricey location down the street from their luxurious offices in New York City, the center of the universe in Jack's mind, though not in Chuck's view. They were like many in their generation who had serial girlfriends but no marriages, as many of their female classmates had serial boyfriends but few marriages.

They were the ying and yang of business life. Jack did the dreaming and selling as the front man; Chuck carried the water and made things work day to day in the back office. People thought of them as the odd couple but didn't seem to realize that their differences meant they never competed for the same things and frankly weren't interested in them. All of this made for a pretty perfect partnership up until recently.

Chuck had forced Jack a few years ago to agree to liquefy their holdings so they each had $250 million out of the company. To please the Board they had done this back in the days at a $5 billion valuation so the company benefited from that sale as it was now worth $16 billion and hopefully more after the Simply news hit the Street.

When the announcement hit the wire, a few minutes later the stock popped up to a $20 billion market cap and everything.com got Simply for free plus an added $2 billion in market cap. Thus it was in the crazy hazy days of the dot com boom on Wall Street.

The Sloan had lined up $2 billion worth of buy orders at the $20 billion market cap price since several funds had no everything.com stock and needed some to keep their percentages in dot coms up, trend right, and please their investors, the most important thing for them. So, Elizabeth smiled upon learning that; she didn't want to hold that loan for long; she was pleased the price was high enough to please the boys as she called them and made a tidy commission for the Sloan.

She texted Chuck the news making Simply free for them and, at the moment, giving them an additional $2 billion market cap boost. She didn't think it would last at that frothy cap, but it was a dot com boom so who knew.

Upon hearing the news, Jack turned to Chuck much like Robert Redford did to his campaign manager in *The Candidate* and said, "What do I do now?"

Chuck smiled, noting the "I" not "we" which Jack had been using of late, and Chuck said, "Time to start your party now, Jack." Jack took the "your" party in stride and smiled.

Jack tended to be secretive about his various goings on despite acting as if it was one happy family. It clearly was a nervous family of late since it had evolved into 24/7 Jack, Jack, Jack.

Chuck saw that baldly; Jack tended to fool himself, keeping his contradictory ideas tidily together, that he could be secretive while openhanded at the same time. Odd, Chuck thought; how well he deluded himself about it too.

He did not fool the others in the company who were frequently made nervous by the impulsive and impetuous Jack. Chuck knew that in Jack's mind what he chose not to see did not exist and that was that, as it always had been. It was that of late Jack chose not to see many more things.

"Great," Jack said with bravado. "I am entering a new period, aren't I? I know, Chuck, you think I should be more defensive. But I won't stand for it. Now is the time to keep charging forward." Chuck had seen the danger up close and personal at his Vermont hideaway. He did not let Jack know he knew about all that nor did Jack comment on it himself. Their divide was broadening by the hour, Jack thought. Well, tonight those hours would be up.

Chuck paused, and said attempting to bridge the yawning gap so Jack would still think he was hopeful, "But will your army follow you? Remember Alexander's that rebelled in India because they realized he wanted to keep charging while they just wanted to go home, enjoy the booty, and smell the flowers with their spoils of war."

"Yes, but that's not for me and they can't stop me," He declared starkly, subtlely pleased that Chuck was still trying. Well, not for long he thought, not for long as he thought he would deal with that tomorrow since something must have gone wrong with his cowboy effort some weeks ago.

Chuck looked at him, seeing that this was the end of things for them together. There would be no getting over it. He smiled carefully as he said, "OK, glad it will work for you. I'll ride the sidecar."

Jack smiled his magnanimous smile and nodded, but the glimmer in his eye indicated to Chuck he wouldn't be riding in that side car for long. "OK, good you are with me on that. I'll call the party for this afternoon at my place. Get it set up with the caterer," as Jack left the room imperially, having treated Chuck as the servant he had become.

Chuck took it while smiling, nodded, and left the room. He spoke briefly with their 4 key people, Bruce Dahl, VP Marketing & Sales, Jane Johnson, CFO, Jackie Marlow, Social Media, and Amar Prince, Data.

None of them seem terribly excited. Well, Chuck thought, this would not be good for them individually. Collectively he was unsure about how things would unfold for them.

That was that for now. Chuck elected to go home to his nearby condo and await the party's beginning next door at Jack's. He had texted the caterer and everything was good to go. They had done this many times before, under less chilly circumstances. This wasn't their first rodeo, but it was a different one.

Now they were done, sort of. But, being only 30, they seemed to have a long way to go in life and Chuck wasn't sure Jack had any idea what a big moment this was for both of them.

Chapter 4

party

Pride before fall.

The party started at 3 PM. Jack came in with the 4 major players who had walked over with him as his entourage. Chuck knew they came in from his hall surveillance camera. He elected to stay put for a while.

About 3 hours later the key 25 people had shown up. Then Chuck moseyed on over, opened Jack's door with the code, and went in to join the gathering. Jack hadn't changed it yet; interesting.

Their core group was there. The party had been going on for some time. Chuck noticed a fair amount of concern among the partygoers related, he was sure, to their "what's next" question so prevalent in dot coms. He noticed the few dot com veterans were less concerned; these were the fatalists. Along for the ride as long as it went; pretty sure it wouldn't be long they suspected. Possibly so, he thought. They'd seen enough upheaval in the dot com boom to think, "What's one more?"

Also of course, the top 4 had plenty of stock for life if the price held up for another few months when the stock vested over $15 billion valuation. The other 25 had enough to each buy a new house if the stock held up. No one else would benefit much and that was why Jack didn't have any of them at the party.

These 29 were tied to Jack. His decisions would impact their lives deeply. Jack liked the power; Chuck knew he liked it too much and could have someone take issue with it. He would be right about that as it turned out.

The dancing and noise continued. Jack had a 2 floor condo so with the party on the upper floor no one below would be disturbed. Next door was Chuck, and he was here so could not be disturbed either. The other side was a glorious view of the Manhattan Skyline. So they could make as much racket as Jack wanted. Most people thought Jack only swaggered; he did so, but carefully as the condo layout was but one example and the carefully selected party attendees another.

The party attendees needed Jack's corporate dance to go on so their stock vested, which he knew. And Jack knew after that there would be a whole new world at everything.com. He had planned for it. What Jack knew, and thought Chuck did not, is that Chuck would no longer be part of it.

2 of the top 4 were now just highly paid staff; Jack had terminated their predecessors 6 months ago when they indicated Jack needed to fix the company or it would spin out of control. Jack squelched rebellions 1 rebel at a time. He got each nicely placed elsewhere, playing paddy cake not hard ball with them. But they were gone and that was the point.

He had termination plans for the other 2 and most of the 25. Chuck knew that Jack had such a plan for him too. Well, that was now, so Chuck could not afford to wait any longer. Even if had just been edged out, and Jack would say it was him or me, the Board would have to back Jack. And that was that.

As the Islamics say, "It is written" and they would be right. The market cap was based on hype that only Jack could provide. Chuck could only provide cashflow and profit, which were not nearly as marketable these days, certainly not at everything.com's inflated market cap.

With those thoughts Chuck thought he should nurse his bourbon tonight to get through all this to the finale. This was a Jack "look at me" party. He would fall in line because despite being boyhood friends, Jack had edged out from that brotherly twosome to be the king pin. And that too was that.

Chuck could tell his sliding fate from the newer hires who just considered him another boss, not a top boss. Well, that was the way it was and Chuck had learned to live with it.

Chuck was standing alone. This had started to happen more and more often of late since people below him didn't consider him part of their group and the top 4 were uncertain. This in fact suited his lone wolf approach to life and had made him far more effective of late, emphasized by bagging the elephant with Simply, and their gold mine of proprietary content and accelerating cashflow with no investment required to maintain the content and little to expand it. The perfect business. Now they owned it; rather Jack and everything.com did.

"Boring, old line serial entrepreneur, cautious, conservative, a lone wolf worker like you, Chuck." Jack had said with disdain about the Simply Founder. He had been right. They were soulmates sharing lone wolf profit oriented canoe guide Thoreauian simplicity, and that was a mouthful to even think about, Chuck thought smiling to himself.

"You'll get on well with him," Jack had said when Chuck first broached the acquisition subject. He was right about that; but also, Jack missed a point: that old guy Brown could teach him a thing or two about streamlining their business.

Brown had already done that just with a few of his throw away lines. Now Chuck could appeal to him for more. Chuck had wisely not introduced him, or Janet the CEO, to Jack. That would have killed the deal for sure.

Chuck knew that Brown thought Jack should be moved out to preserve the company but didn't expect it to happen, indicated by his only accepting an all cash offer. Did Jack get that? Chuck didn't know.

Chuck had unconsciously gotten a second bourbon to stimulate his thinking, though he knew he always paid the price for it the next day. That was a point, wasn't it? But Chuck needed to get through this.

Jack and he didn't even pretend to talk as they used to do. It was like a hot romance that had turned into a boring marriage. And as the richer husband in that situation, Jack had started to withhold what he really thought about things. But Chuck did too, to extend the metaphor, to his being the subordinate wife.

Chuck could tell everyone had prepared in their own way for this party. They knew everything.com had a new more reliable stream of cash from Simply. It would be the company's own little bank, a bank they didn't have to answer to but could take all their money, stripping them as clean as a Safeway chicken. And yes, Chuck thought, they were correct they could get away with it if things stayed the same. But they wouldn't, which the other party goers didn't know.

Chuck admired Warren Buffett, a man and thinking Jack despised because it was all about measurable financial value which offended Jack's sense of real value, hype, and market cap.

Chuck's favorite Buffett line was, "First you make a judgment about the value; later you weigh the earnings and cashflow." Well, Chuck had weighed Simply earnings and they had no debt and $100 million annual cashflow growing 20% per year with no end in sight. Also, importantly, the brand and the content shrieked out value at a low cost to the consumer with delivery seamlessly and virtually free through downloads, the coming thing worldwide.

Check that he thought. Already worldwide, just that most of the world didn't have a lot of money. Most importantly, mobile was picking up momentum in the rich markets of the US, UK, Germany, and Japan which Simply near free audiobooks and eBooks were perfect for.

Chuck sighed. The bartender thought it was the bourbon. No, it was Chuck thinking about Simply as a Mozart of business as long as it didn't get messed up. He never understood why Coke or Proctor & Gamble had armies of people when the brands were what mattered.

They got 80% market share when priced like their competitors. With their volume they could easily do that but elected not to do so. Simply had done that and gone a step further, priced lower than their competitors so saw their cashflow and market share grow, grow, grow seemingly effortlessly.

Well, Simply had done it right. He would like to ride that wave, from the top now. But he knew that wouldn't happen because once before when he had tried to take a smaller piece and go out on his own Jack had said, "No, Chuck, I need that part of the business. You can't do that."

Chuck had come to realized that once Jack had sold the sizzle the steak would be enough and Chuck could go along without Jack. It had been a profound moment as those moments are. It was clear that only one of them could win out and Jack had the rail.

With that Chuck got a third and last bourbon so he could work the party for his ends. Chuck was a handsome six footer with kind eyes that women liked so he never had any trouble attracting nice ones. And pretty ones. The hot numbers liked him and the smart ones trusted him. It was just part of being Chuck so he was largely unaware of this.

He had no interest in conquering women or putting notches on his belt. He liked them and often that was quite enough for him, though not always for them. But as one woman said, "Chuck, a girl can rest with you. It is nice." He had always wondered about that; when he told other women about that comment, they nodded knowingly. Seeing that, he learned to use it for a mellow time with women.

Tonight was no exception. Chuck was someone people instantly respected and trusted, hence no one had felt required to come over and talk him up. They would wait for him to make his gentlemanly rounds which he always did, with tonight being no exception.

He talked to each person about their interests. He danced with a few and drank no more. And generally partied on. He was a good dancer so always found women to dance with.

He had noticed that Jack had cut one of the women out and gone towards the back bedroom to descend the stairs to bed her. Jack always did this in such a way as to appear private but show off his new trophy at the same time, not an easy thing to pull off, Chuck thought. Jack was not a particularly handsome man or at ease with women. So displaying them was important to him.

Well, that was that for Jack tonight. About an hour later when the party was going at full tilt without people being concerned the big boss was around, and Kit Miller, his latest squeeze, was occupied dancing with another, Chuck drifted off to the rear bathroom. Chuck returned to the party 9 minutes later. No one missed him because the party was in full swing and most had had more than enough to drink. The party was going full swing as Kit was still dancing happily with the guy Chuck had left her with.

More people had drifted in, people personally connected to the 29 already there. Chuck suspected they had texted them once Jack left; he would be right about that. They knew Jack was fun-loving on the surface but could take offense quickly and permanently in an instant. They also knew that although Jack gave an open party invitation, they had to be on the doorman's list or approved by Jack before entering.

Jack was always careful about that as about many things he thought others didn't notice. He never seemed to realize everyone took his temperature because he could suddenly promote, fire, exile, or destroy a career.

Yes, Chuck thought, for Jack's security that doorman list made sense. It was a good idea because Jack had made many enemies in his life, primarily on purpose Chuck knew. With that in mind, he patiently waited a couple of hours or so for the party to wind down enough that Kit would want to go back to his condo to crash for the night.

In the meantime, Chuck drifted around the party to be seen but not heard other than with a nod or laugh, tipping of the head or clinking of drink glasses.

As Tolstoy had said, he reflected, time and patience are the ultimate warriors. Well, Chuck let them work for him that night as the hours drifted away until the early morning hours when Kit gave him the high sign and they left for his place next door.

By then most people had left so the remaining ones took a cue from their leaving and did so shortly after Kit and Chuck went back to his place.

In his condo, he poured his fourth bourbon and a glass of Shiraz for Kit. Some minutes later they went comfortably off to bed together. He had no landlines to ring and always turned off all his devices when a woman was with him so they had a peaceful sleep until later that morning.

He woke up by being shaken by Kit, who said, "Jack died last night."

"Jack?"

Kit continued, "Carla just texted me. She was scared to death waking up next to a dead man she hardly knew. Now what?"

Chapter 5

night before

A journey of 1000 miles starts with a single step

When Jack had cut out his new girl, making a show of it, Chuck had gone an hour later to the rear bathroom. He used the listening device he had planted in Jack's room and heard gentle snores, a deeper male one and a lighter female one.

With that signal, Chuck descended the stairs, used the special code to open the door, and went along the corridor to Jack's room. Upon entering he saw them rather restlessly asleep.

Jack always kept a handy glass of water next to his side of the bed to knock back after a few hours' sleep to help him hydrate for a better work morning as he put it. Chuck had picked up the habit which worked well for him too.

Today it would be Jack's doom as Chuck poured the colorless poison in his glass which was enough to kill 3 mules he had figured. He also took Jack's cell phone and nearby laptop.

With that, Chuck left the room, went upstairs, and removed the video tape from the security camera of the evening's goings on. He opened the safe and removed everything but Jack's will and their buy/sell agreement which, in effect, gave the stock tax free to the other upon a death. He read the will and saw that it remained the same, stating that he, Chuck, was the executor and sole beneficiary since Jack had no family or friends other than Chuck, and some friend he turned out to be Chuck thought.

His money motive was clear but would be obscured by the fact he had plenty already. But best he be prepared he had considered, chuckling about the Boy Scout motto of that title.

He removed the hard drive from Jack's PC, replacing it with another, pocketing the several flash drives from the safe and Jack's cell, and a few papers he folded and put in his pocket. He was pleased to see there were no bulges. He had worn a loose fitting jacket to provide for a little extra luggage, as he thought of it.

He then returned to the party. Chuck had only been gone about 9 minutes. No one seemed to have missed him and why should they? He had stood by behind the door back to the party for 15 seconds or so to get his game face on, chill down, motor down, and otherwise think party not killing. It worked he thought, as he strolled into the party and purposefully went on a wandering diagonal so as not to appear headed for anything, which in fact he was not.

He fixed himself a light bourbon and water so as to appear occupied. One of their party innovations was to allow people to pour their own drinks if they chose not to use the bartender. With the mixed drinks they had learned that some people liked to coach others so that worked too.

In fact, many dating contacts were made that way as women selected a man they thought they might like and asked him to make them a special drink. Sometimes they drank it and sometimes they didn't. Men liked this approach because they could feel competent, helpful, and nice all at the same time. Women liked it because they could appraise the man in the process.

Chuck had discovered that most younger men had learned to let women do the choosing, which put less stress on the men and simplified things for them. There were enough attractive single women in New York that men could wait for the next one. It probably made things tougher on men in Grand Rapids and such places but Chuck wasn't there nor were his colleagues. In reading John Cheever stories, he had realized it probably had always been this way as Manhattan had always been a chick magnet, to use the modern lingo.

He was thinking about this as a semi-drunk colleague was talking mildly to himself and Chuck about some story from long ago that neither would remember in 15 minutes. It was companionable as this guy always was. Tommy Frank, the companionable guy, had long liked and admired Chuck. They seemed to have a casual and happy relationship that both could rely upon. That was good for them both now, though, of course, for different reasons.

Chuck seemed preoccupied so Tommy knew the formula, tell a light story, smile, chuckle, and enjoy the time together. This had worked before and was now, especially since Tommy needed a bit of time to sober up so he could stagger home, about 6 blocks away. Chuck looked content so Tommy went on with his story.

He wound down gently and they sat there quietly for a bit. Tommy was thinking about his walk home. Chuck was remembering Winesburg, Ohio, and the moments in one's life that came and passed quickly, never to be recaptured or altered.

He knew he just had one of them. He said a few words to Tommy about his upcoming stagger, which got a chuckle out of Tommy and created a memory Chuck thought would stick. He would be right.

Kit came over to him and pulled him on the dance floor. Chuck was a good dancer so it went well. Kit was cute so Tommy would remember this too, Chuck thought. He would be right about that also.

The evening or rather the early morning drifted on as Chuck stayed with it until Kit wanted to leave and they went to his place.

He wanted to settle her down so gave her a glass of Shiraz. She drank about half on her side of the bed and started to nod off. They crashed pleasantly for the night as Chuck wondered how

the news would come his way about the death, as he sipped his
last   bourbon   by   his   bedside.

Chapter 6

first reckoning

When you think you have a man in the palm of your hand count your fingers

Kit repeated herself, "Now what, Jack? We can't just sit here."

Actually they were lying there and Chuck didn't want to be a pedant by pointing that out, but it was a boulder in his way. He roused himself, "What did you text back?"

"Nothing yet. But I feel I should."

"Then do so."

"What do I say?"

"Kit, that depends on you. I would think she should call the police and let them take it from there, but she has to decide that for herself."

Kit looked at him harshly, "But you were his friend and partner, and we were with him last night." She wound down a bit and just looked at him before going on, "That's it?"

"Kit, what can I do? Jack has been core to my life since college. If I could do something for Jack I would, but I can't. Anything I do now is for someone else, not Jack. I'll miss him; I'll have to get used to that somehow. Perhaps I will never really get used to him being gone. Everything we did together is now changed. I don't know how exactly." He paused to let her take over the conversation.

"Well, I am going over there for Carla," as she got up to go. "Aren't you coming?"

"No. You deal with Carla. Jack is gone so I can't help him, as I just said. I have to think about the others, especially at the Company since he was the front man."

"Sounds harsh."

"It is harsh. Jack was the front man as is a maître d. Customers don't see the chef. I was the back office, like the chef. Now I have to do my back office job and fill in the front until the company finds someone else. And they will never find another Jack. So that's what I have to do now. You deal with Carla or not. I'll have to go in. Most people will have hangovers and more, after that brawl last night; so that will help a bit," he mused.

Kit got up, put her clothes on, and went to the bathroom. When he heard the shower he popped in and said, "I'm going over to the office. See you there," and left before hearing her reply.

Chuck had gone over his prospective day early in the morning as well as on his short walk to the office. He entered and it was obvious everyone knew. He had decided his best move was to act as a grieved friend trying to right the ship.

The stock had crashed over 50% already that morning, bringing the market cap down to $9 billion. Chuck, as a high Machiavellian, knew that the market had declared the company worth $11 billion less without Jack, essentially because they considered him irreplaceable.

The smart move for him was to let it be so. He knew that Jack had been hyping and hyping the stock until it was in the stratosphere; that was his doing and Chuck would let it be so.

2 business reporters from *The Wall Street Journal* were waiting for him. They knew him and both had had their issues with everything.com's market value. They both had written that Chuck was a good carpenter but not the person to build the

whole house. They had both from time to time criticized Jack on other grounds.

So, in short, they had been generally negative and dissatisfied with the 2 principals and that sold papers and got attention. Praise was nice but like good weather, ignored; storms were watched, whether in weather or corporate life. They lived for the negative in other words. And they were here to find it. Chuck couldn't fan those flames but he would let them do so since driving down the stock price suited his purposes.

They were surprised to get an immediate interview. One said simply, "Why?"

Chuck said, "You represent *The Wall Street Journal* and have a deep knowledge of the company; you have had a generally dim view of many things about us and your readers are looking for your take on things with Jack's sudden death. All as it should be," and he paused.

They looked at him and he went on, "Why don't we order lunch in and talk some more. What will you have?" as he reached for his scratch pad and took their orders. He pushed a hotlink to the downstairs deli, placed their orders as well as his usual, smiled, and paused again.

"It has been a tough day already and I just got here. I'll have a little pick me up, I think," as he went to the liquor cabinet, waved them over, and they all had something. With that the conversation began again, albeit more gently and slowly. A man providing a carte blanche lunch and liquor was not to be sneered at, at least not while still drinking his liquor and eating his food.

"So now?"

Chuck took a breath and said, "So now I go and try to put humpty dumpty back together again," and they had their headline. "Jack pushed for growth; my job was the bottom line. So I'll do what I am good at and build the bottom line."

"But the stock price might tank."

"It already has 55% according to the last quote," as he pointed to the screen posting it in real time. "My job will be to stabilize things. With that gentleman, I have to get to work. Enjoy the drinks and food when it arrives. I'll be back to get my share." Just then the food came in and they all sat down quietly together and had their lunch or dinner for them and breakfast for Chuck.

After finishing, Chuck got up and left them to it. He could move quickly and quietly when he wanted to do so, and did then. He was gone in their mid-bite, so to speak.

Chapter 7

journal's reckoning

It isn't hold em or fold em; it is freeze and run

Chuck left the offices at that point. He told the general manager on the way out he was doing so.

The GM said, "What now Chuck?"

"Business as usual, pal. Just do your job; pass the word to others to do theirs. I'll be back tomorrow after mulling things over tonight and grieving for my oldest friend."

The day before when Chuck knew the party would be coming up to celebrate the close with Simply, he had announced a 2 week electronics off vacation for himself. This was customary in the company and appreciated by one and all. Since it was also established that the vacationer would, on the honor system, open emails only once every 3 days but would still not be responsible to answer them, he would follow that routine to the letter or rather, as he chuckled to himself, to the email.

With that comment to the GM just then that he was going home to grieve, he left the premises by the back way to avoid any reporters hovering outside. Jack and he had learned a route through their office building basement that went to the abutting building so they could go out that back door, walk over to their own, and come in unannounced up the service elevator which stopped at their floor but only had two condos and no one else had the code to stop the elevator on the floor. No handymen to trade the code for something else; only them.

As with most secrets, they are only secret if one person knows them. As with many things now, only Chuck knew the code to the floor. He was totally safe here. To get a warrant and up here would be tough. Because the police had been involved, he had given the doorman early that morning a onetime 24 hour code for them to Jack's, as Jack and he had done for others in the past that needed access. Each code would deactivate automatically within 24 hours for security purposes. He withheld a code, 24 hour or otherwise, to his own condo entrance from the hall on their floor.

This time he had come back to his condo by the service elevator, letting himself in with his code so as not to appear on any surveillance cameras in the regular passenger elevator or have any record there. Jack and he kept a SUV in a garage 5 blocks away under a different name. He planned to start his 2 week vacation tomorrow by driving it out of town at 3 AM the next morning to Newport, Vermont to his cabin there and use a hidden canoe to cross the lake to Quebec the next night.

They had a tent and sleeping bags in the SUV, provisions, and more, so they could do this kind of thing that they wished they could have done in their youth but didn't have the money to do so. Now when they could afford it, they rarely could afford the time to do it. It sounded like an O'Henry story, he thought.

Chuck was going to do it now though since he had the time and the money at long last, as well as the freedom to do so without bad consequences except for possibly the police.

Jack and he had soundproofed their condos so he heard nothing of what might be going on next door by the police or anyone else that afternoon and evening. At 2:45 AM the next morning his cell alarm rang, he got a few things, and left down the service elevator again. For fun and safety, he had put on a theatrical disguise complete with a false beard, wig, and floppy hat. He had also put on elevator shoes to make him 6' 3" not 6' tall. Small differences, but why not? Safer.

He knew the theatrics distracted him from the seriousness of it all. Quite a parallel he mused. By then he was on the street going towards the garage. He arrived about 15 minutes later, got in the SUV, and started it. It was a small dated commercial building so didn't have many spots or any security cameras, which they had both liked. He pressed the garage door opener and was off.

It was a 7 hour drive up to Newport on Lake Mem as he called it. The official Indian name was a 2 county name, starting in one and ending in another. It was not only long but unpronounceable too. It was a pretty straight shot. Up the Thruway to Albany, cut over on Route 7, and then up 91 to just before Newport, where he took a short ride on Route 191 west to the Newport area. His property was on the lake off Bluff Road. It was only a couple of miles to the Canadian border across the middle of the lake. He had a submergible he used to occasionally cross unseen. He had another place south of Magog, Quebec which he could land at underwater, which was pretty cool. So no one knew if he was there or not.

He had a car there and could leave on Route 10 to go west to the rest of Canada. Chuck thought he would stay bunkered down in the Magog place for a week or so and see how that went.

He stopped at the Lebanon Municipal Airport and got a *The Wall Street Journal* from their coin news box. The market cap had fallen to $6 billion and stabilized there. Good, he thought. $6 billion was a fair price; $20 billion was ridiculous.

Since he now owned and controlled 60% of the stock, he had a $3.6 billion net worth in everything.com and about $1 billion outside it. Even at just 3% interest that was over $100 million per year, far more than he ever would need, and the company was depreciated because of Jack not any of Chuck's doings other than the murder. As long as he kept clear of that he would be fine forevermore. Step 1 was business as usual.

He read the headline:

Newberg Trying to Put Humpty Dumpty Back Together Again.

Chuck Newberg, Jack Towson's partner at everything.com, told *Journal* reporters that his job was to put Humpty Dumpty back together again. Chuck is a workman like COO but no Towson, as Chuck was the first to admit. Chuck said he could understand the market knocking the stock down yesterday but he would try to help the stock price by increasing earnings. Chuck admitted that he was not a rainmaker but said the company would undoubtedly seek one, though he said he was doubtful they could find anyone like Jack. That is an understatement from his longtime friend, Harvard College and Business School roommate, and business partner. When asked what he would do now Chuck replied, "Business as usual."

Not very promising for the stockholders who bought into the growth story. But we will see.

The story went on from there speaking to making stock options worthless which might cause an exodus of the talent that made everything.com what it was, the loss of value to Chuck himself, the loss to the institutions invested in the company, and more along that vein. They did everything but put a black border around the column, Chuck chuckled.

With that Chuck crafted a press release to counter *The Wall Street Journal's* premise about the demise of the company, but support their point that the hype days were over and presumably the momentum investors would bail out then.

Chuck Newberg, CEO of everything.com, announced that he would stabilize the company through emphasizing earnings such as the $100 million from Simply, their latest acquisition, pare back their speculative investments for the future, and deliver another $400 million in pretax, to create a $350 million total after tax annual earnings which would support a $10 billion or more market cap at a roughly 30 PE.

34

Chuck sent this to the everything.com General Manager for immediate release, which meant 9 AM.

Chuck decided to rest at his Newport cabin that night as planned before pushing off the next day.

The next morning he learned that the news release had stabilized the stock at slightly less than a $6 billion market cap. The follow-up article by the 2 *Journal* newsies had a sizzling headline:

Newberg pushes an earnings not growth story at
everything.com.

Everyone knows you buy P & G, IBM, and Exxon for earnings. You buy dotcoms for growth. So Newberg plans to have an earnings company in the unstable dot com business. That left a ho hum in the marketplace, though the stock drifted back up to a $6 billon market cap where it will probably stay for some time.

"Perfect," Jack said out loud trying to contain himself, getting breakfast, and walking around his property sight unseen.

Chapter 8

police

Speak softly but carry a big stick

As a high profile case, Centre Street sent out their top detective, George Parsons, along with Joyce Allison, who had all the educational credentials to become Commissioner some day and much of the moxie too. This team had cracked several tough cases. The Commissioner hoped this would be a success too as a high profile murder case.

George and Joyce arrived together. George told Joyce, "This is your world. Have a good look into your world as a person not a cop. You are going to see things none of the rest of us will. And when you become Commissioner, remember me," and he laughed. She smiled but was a bird dog at heart, raring to get after it, and George liked that about her too.

"Joyce, I am going to stay down here in the lobby. Text me when ready. Scout out the place. Take your time; be patient. See what you see. Try to visualize it all. You should take the lead on this one. OK?"

"Thanks George."

"No, thank you. This promises to be a tough one. We are talking complicated motives; high end people; your Ivy League/Manhattan world. Nothing to be disparaged. But something to be alert to in order to solve, if we can."

"You sound discouraged. Why?"

"The obvious motives don't apply. Jack, the victim, didn't have a jealous wife or girlfriend; he didn't even have an ex-wife which so many have. Jack's death cost everyone at the party money, with the market cap going down by 55% in one day, then another 30% or so today already. So the majority of people with stock options are underwater or took a serious bath."

"Carla, the girl in bed with him, was traumatized. She is a heads up young woman who called me back on the phone to report what she knew which wasn't much. Then we have her friend, Kit, in bed with the other partner, Chuck. She said she was a light sleeper and he was in bed all night. The partner lost 55% of his stock value in one day, and another 30% today. I am told it will go lower yet. Yes, he evidently inherits from Jack, but even with that he lost half the value and, according to everyone, that's billions with a B. And they have been lifelong friends with no arguments noted in any record. And to make it worse, they each had different talents so the partner has to fill a big gap. Finally, the victim has no living relatives. Now that's rare to have everyone lose by a death. So that's why I am not optimistic, Joyce."

"George, it would have taken me days to say that, if I could have figured it out. I take your point; we should think of this as a no-win case so any flicker is a bright sign." George nodded as she went on. "And you think I might be able to come up with a motive. No. What you mean is I might have the best chance so you are giving me a clear field by saying no solution, fine; any suggestion of a solution, Eureka."

George smiled, "Exactly."

"I am a pretty good student George," she said relaxing.

"That you are. That you are. Go to it. I'm going to walk around and think about it; play cop if I can find an affordable donut in this neighborhood, which I doubt," and he smiled as he waved her on to the elevator.

The door man was elegant, clearly more than a doorman. He looked at her somewhat quizzically due to her Park Avenue clothes doing police work. It clashed; he was right of course.

37

She knew from long experience how to get him to talk and that was by not asking questions, not now. Let him relax; let him decide; if he decides to speak she will learn things; if not she won't; but if she started with questions she would be misled, possibly skillfully so. She knew how to relax in an elevator and did so. On the sixth floor, he let her off and then into the victim's apartment on the left.

This floor had been totally cleaned up before they got the call from Carla, the girl in bed. It looked like a studio set; well, as she took a turn in the living room, it was a studio set, that of a young rich nouveau money guy, though in brains, which he had in abundance from all reports.

She wrote down her thoughts. A studio set. Totally an alpha male place with all utilitarian stuff, no frills or nesting, no personal things, no photographs, and lots of open space that men like. Totally a man's place. Not a touch of woman anywhere. A great party place which it was and had been last night.

She went through the door to the back. On the left were several bathrooms, clearly set up for women. All the fixings inside from women's things to aspirin, Tylenol, and more legal OTC drugs such as Claritin. She noticed the portraits of ladies on the doors--Jane Austen, several female movie stars, and a young girl who looked like she might be Eleanor Roosevelt as a child.

On the other side were pictures of Socrates, Dickens, Twain, and a few male movie stars. Inside were urinals, she had never seen those before in a private house. Various medicines, cigars, cigarettes, and a large refrigerator with beer and wine. Quite the bathroom; could stay in here for a day or two; well there were some chairs so maybe some did.

Behind that were several bedrooms, clearly available for anyone who couldn't make it home or was invited to just stay over. A small kitchen with easy to use things such as a deluxe coffee maker, microwave, dry cereals, fruits, and such things in the refrigerator. The freezer had Birdseye Fresh vegetables for easy heating, a few other frozen meals, juices, and more. A great place to visit or stay she thought. Bountiful but impersonal. She hadn't seen a personal touch yet.

She went downstairs and found a living room, office which was spare as well, a well-stocked library with books that had clearly been read, music, movies, and more. Several more bedrooms. His was spare; no photos, trophies, or other personal objects. Looked more like a guy who was a camper, which she knew from his bio he was. Spare, the operable word and description of his space. The room was incredibly neat for most men, but not his kind, the guide type who only took what they could carry. She had known a few of those in her day.

They seemed simple but never were. No, it was that they tried to act simple and usually succeeded on the surface but never really were. That was it.

In fact, as she recalled, they were the only men who tried to sell her on being simple, not deep or important or anything but simple. That was the clue of course; they were hiding in the open, and most of them did a good job of it until she got to know them better.

A thought flashed across her mind from her own experience with these kinds of men. He may have pushed someone's buttons and pushed them in a way he did not recognize or fear. He may have been a truth teller who told a truth to someone who couldn't tolerate hearing it. He may have stepped across some boundary, that must be it if not love, money, jealousy, power, or family.

Well, as her favorite fiction detective Jane Marple had said, who did he remind her of?

She had had a budding relationship with a self-sufficient guy, yes, she thought, that was it. Self-sufficient; totally sufficient to himself no matter how much he liked or even needed other people.

They were getting serious and she started to argue with him once, just once, and not talk. He had looked at her long and hard; she wasn't quite sure why because she had committed other presumed female transgressions before such as talking too much about herself, being late, saying the wrong things to some of his friends, and such breaches of male decorum.

She felt a cold wind come over her from him. She let it pass. He was polite. He worked himself up to be politer. He struggled and got back to warm. But he didn't get hot or touch her again that night, not even a goodnight kiss.

He never called or wrote again. She finally cornered him at an event and asked what happened and he said, "You crossed a line; you started to argue; I don't deal well with that so I retreated."

She tried to explain. And tried some more. He had finally told her, "Joyce, it isn't you; it is me." Every woman knows that line. It is the end, the dead-end of all dead-ends with men. She said she appreciated it and staggered off never to repeat that with that kind of man again.

The second incident happened when she got tight with a guy as they had a rollicking good time. She was feeling possessive in a foursome and asked if she could have something from his plate. He said no, but he would be happy to get her another plate.

She said, "That's stupid, just a taste," and took it. She never heard from him again.

When she cornered him at a gathering they accidently met at he had said, "You didn't want a bite, you wanted an easement."

She denied it vehemently until they separated at the party they had separately attended. Then she realized he had been right.

She was trying to show possession and he didn't like that. Not the least little bit.

Both of these men had had apartments like this one but on a smaller scale. It struck her, too, that this larger apartment had to have more stuff so those traits wouldn't have been too obvious to others. She also remembered that neither of those guys wanted her to come to their place. They preferred hers or to travel somewhere else. Then she realized they had never bed her in their places. She had forced her way in subtly on a pretext and that was that. When they entertained they took people out and paid for them generously. They hadn't had her over to dinner though both were more than adequate cooks and did so willingly at her place.

They also brought the food; just the right amount as if on a camping or canoe trip. Never any leftovers. Yes, that was it.

She went over to the refrigerator. Yep, he bought by the meal, not food. She looked in the garbage; nothing. Even the recycling area had nothing even though the refrigerator was full of things that would be recycled.

Yep. She knew her guy.

The question was who ate off his plate that he couldn't get rid of? Or who argued with him? That seemed more likely given his wealth. An investor? A patent holder? A partner? Ah, she needed to meet them to test her theory.

But there was a missing piece. She was describing why he would push someone away not why someone else would do it to him. Ah, but she remembered those 2 guys had had friends just like them. So maybe he did it to a likeminded person. That was her best bet, she concluded.

She needed to make a list of people who he couldn't get rid of and he might have pushed too far. Investors? Yep. Patent holder. Not likely, but maybe. Irreplaceable employee?

41

Unlikely given he was a salesman extraordinaire. Partner? Yes. The most likely if he was like the victim.

Well, he had a partner and they had known each other forever; perhaps it was like one of those 50 year marriages where one person finally can't stand it anymore and blows the other person's head off. It happens. She had already witnessed the devastating results of one: one spouse dead, the other in jail for life. The interesting point was the person in jail seemed accepting of their fate as if better than having continued as things were. In short, jail was better than their old life.

This murder had something of that feeling about it. She would talk to George about all of this now that she had a feel for the situation and personality of the victim.

Chapter 9

police plan

An army moves on its stomach

Joyce told George her theory. George thought about it for a few minutes before speaking and then said, "Interesting eliminations, Joyce. It has the right kind of feel to it. Makes no sense in a way; but nothing makes more sense. And that often leads to a perpetrator. Solid work."

Joyce knew not to use an aw shucks approach with George. As he often said, they shouldn't be married to her idea but it was the best they had at the moment and that was good enough for now. As he had taught her, this was a good way to start and keep an open mind about what else popped up.

Joyce then said, "What do you think we should do now? Find and interview him? Find others first? What?"

"Best to find out where he is. He's a planner; he will have a plan. We have to figure that out first, long before we move in on him in any way. We don't want to tip him off to our interest. The office is just 4 blocks away. Let's walk over and find out who is there. That will give us a beginning. Your idea is growing on me, Joyce. Well nothing else is so let's go with it," as he chuckled. "Stay loose. We aren't married to it as I have said to you before about a good idea. But it is interesting and that guy, if not the guy, might well take us to another who is the perpetrator."

"George, the forensic people said Jack took the poison at about 3 AM. The body was discovered by Carla about 10 AM. She texted her friend, Kit, who was in bed with the partner. Chuck apparently took it in stride as he does everything with a 'what's done is done' attitude according to her. He said he was going to the office to deal with things. We will see."

"Joyce, she was forthright with me. What did you think of Carla?"

"Smart cookie; doing well at the company; well liked, pretty as you would expect if in bed with the big cheese though he was not a handsome man from his photos. His partner is. Stunning in fact but doesn't seem to preen himself about it; takes it in stride as he seems to do with everything else. These kinds of guys are; I have dealt with 2 personally."

George looked at her briefly. Ah, she not only had a professional insight but a personal one as well. In his mind that increased the probability she was right because she was the least prejudiced, side taking person he had ever worked with. Well, ever known in fact. He congratulated himself on not thinking his personal intervention would have helped; it wouldn't have. That was something he learned from his first boss, "Don't think you are the cat's pajamas; don't overestimate your own importance."

When they got to the office, they only got as far as the lobby. With no human there he used the intercom because the door was locked to the inner offices. He asked to the anonymous voice that answered to speak to Chuck or whoever was in charge.

He noticed the place sounded quiet on the speaker's end, as well as in the empty lobby. Interesting no one was in the lobby and the speaker's end was quiet too. He had known founders who had died and lots of grief, or none at all. This was the first time it was this quiet though. He would have to learn more about that. Fast he thought, fast.

The intercom said the GM would come out to see him and quickly went off the device. When he came out he was older than George expected, older than the 2 partners. He looked like a GE guy. He would ask if given an opening.

"Hi, I'm George Parsons from Centre Street and this is my associate Joyce Allison," and he paused. The GM waited. George thought, must be a GE guy because he can hold his counsel.

"We wanted to speak with Chuck Newberg," and paused again.

The GM waited.

"Is he here?"

"No."

"You are being curt."

He paused; no response so he had to go on, "You have had a murder and we are the investigators," at which the GM nodded, "and we would like some information."

No response.

So George continued, "Can we come in and sit down?" The GM sat down in the lobby; he didn't say no, but he did sit down. They joined him.

"Were you at the party last night?"

"Yes."

"What happened?"

"It was just a party. Nothing in particular happened, nothing out of the ordinary that I recall."

"What time did you arrive and leave?"

"I arrived about 5 PM and left at about 1 AM."

"A long time."

"Yes."

"Where is Chuck?"

"On vacation."

"Where?"

"I don't know."

"Why not?

"Company policy."

"Can you tell me what that is?"

"Better that you read it."

"I would like to hear it from you."

"Understood." And the GM was silent.

"Well?"

"Here is a copy of the policy," as he gave it to George. It read as follows:

Vacations are for Vacation

1. Do not call in. Check your email only once every 3 days.

2. If someone is urgently trying to reach you, let me know by email and I will take care of it.

3. Enjoy your time; sit on the beach, climb tall mountains, or just crash. Whatever suits your fancy.

"This is highly unusual," George said. Silence. So he went on. "When did you learn Chuck would be on vacation now?"

"A week ago."

"Do you know where he is going?"

"No."

"By the way, what is your name and title?"

"Jim Johnson, CFO."

"We need to get hold of him. How do we do that?"

"Send an email request to me and I'll forward it to him," and he gave George a card with a general HR email address at the company.

"We can't wait 3 days." Silence.

"Can you do anything else?"

"Put what you want in the email; I will forward it to him."

"Well, Jim, you have me licked for now. I am going to leave now and come back when fortified." Silence.

George stomped out. Joyce smiled at Jim; shook his hand and said, "Thank you."

He nodded; when George had gone out the door he added, "You are welcome," turned on his heel and left the opposite way, by the intercom and out of the lobby. She noticed he used a key to get back in the office.

Outside at the elevator George was fuming. She put her finger to her mouth in the whisper mode and they went down silently together.

Once outside she said, "Let's have our late lunch. It is 3 PM now."

She headed for a pub. George said, "You must have read my mind."

"Yes, have a pop; have 2; then we can talk. But drink something first. That was something and we need to reflect upon   it."   They   did.

Chapter 10

mobile force

Know thy Enemy.

Joyce wouldn't let George get started until he chugged down 2 pints of Guinness. He was ready she thought. He loved working with Joyce; she was better than a wife or a girlfriend. She was a great pal; he'd never had a female pal before and really liked it.

When a colleague said how great looking she was he was surprised, but made no comment. He didn't see her through that lens at all. She was a great pal.

"OK, shoot."

"First, start eating that burger I ordered for you to get you happier and lay a foundation for your third Guinness. You need some happiness fuel before we start in again. And after that you'll go home mellow and cogitate all night and really come up with something."

He looked uncertain as she went on to say, "everything.com is a mobile force. That's what we have to understand. They are everywhere and nowhere. No physical facilities other than a few pop up offices as I call them; that means they could close one and move out overnight. In fact they might and what could we do about it? Zero, nada, nothing. OK we could bark a bit. But to who? Why? Got it?"

"No. That will take a third. And the burger. And some serious naptime. No. I need to stop, drop, and roll, fireman style." George said in a subdued voice.

"Yes. God, George; they may actually move; then what do we do?"

"OK, who else is on the list?"

"You said VC; they had a VC back in the day that made a bundle off them and still may again somehow, the Sloan. In fact they too are a mobile force, having evacuated the US for Dublin. The Senate tried to stop them and were helpless. What is it George?" as she saw him smiling for the first time today.

"The Sloan. My old Pal John Putnam Thatcher, Chairman of the Board now, but SVP back when I knew him. He is a legend in the police business. Ever hear of him?"

"Yes, but I thought it was legendary..."

"Yes and no. Yes it is legendary and no he is real too. He has unraveled a few over the years; unlike that tight ass guy we talked to, John opens them up like a can of worms." He was warming to the task.

Joyce paused, "I'll bet he only opens them up to help the Sloan, and get their money, right?"

"Yes. He is expert at cutting through the emotions etc., and so on, and getting down to the money that is at the root of it, which leads to the emotions etc. He can explain it better than I can. Well, we need to call John. I remember he has a daughter who pulled off the Dublin move and backed doored a murder solution of her own."

George went on, "Backdoored. Well, unlike John, her father, she is more liberal shall we say about handing murderers over to the police. She finds out and they rarely survive her finding out, but she only works to get the money unlike her father who is plain curious though will never admit it, and always turned over the murderer. The police like him; he is like a great drug. Once on a case you want him on more; once on a case you start thinking and talking like him. He is a drug," and George reminisced pleasantly to himself.

Joyce tried to find a number for them and couldn't. The best she could do is call Dublin but it was late at night there. At the same time, George went into his dilapidated little phone book and found Thatcher's home number. He called it.

The phone rang and was picked up with, "Hello."

"Mr. Thatcher, this is Detective George Parsons we worked on a case together. Ah you remember ... well I need to speak with you ... yes it is about the everything.com situation. Day after tomorrow at your place at the Devonshire is fine; no 5 PM is fine; we will wait until then. Yes, we will enjoy a drink or 2 and dinner; thank you for suggesting that incentive. Good night, Sir, and thank you."

"Great. When he sees you, he will get Trinkam. He's the President now but more importantly he is the in-house expert on women. Never married, does a miss on that; but John's Harvard roommate, Tom Robichaux, gets married routinely but somehow escapes with his hide. Of course he has a lot of hide to escape with, financial hide that is."

Joyce saw he remembered them fondly. That was good; hopefully Thatcher felt the same way. It seemed so since he would be offering drinks and dinner; on the other hand, he might be setting the table for some serious evasion. Well, they would see. tomorrow.

Joyce paused before saying, "Robichaux, Devane & Thatcher? They are the #1 boutique investment broker with only a few people. Is the Thatcher related?"

"Yes, he is a Robichaux/Trinkam type, but more like Trinkam. A partier but financially conservative. Rare combination. He, too, has never married, though you might be the one. Now Joyce don't look at me like that. He is the real deal. John's son and supposedly also a chip off the old block too."

51

With that they sat back with their thoughts. George was hopeful; Joyce just opened Pandora's Box; she would see where it led her. A rich presumably fun, financially conservative partier was good for lots of things. She hummed unknowingly.

George noticed and smiled. Well at least one nice thing might come out of this mess. George thought she deserved better than some of the crumb bums, at least in his opinion, she had dealt with as dates. Of course he was prejudiced; but so what? He was entitled, as he quaffed his third Guinness.

He noticed Joyce looked a bit worried, so he asked her why. "George, they are a mobile force. They can do a lot before the day after tomorrow at 5 PM when we meet with Thatcher."

"They may be mobile, but they aren't that mobile to move out and sell off things by then," he chuckled. George would be wrong   about   that.

Chapter 11

sale & buyback

Reach and grab works for me

The Wall Street Journal headline the next morning indicated how wrong George was:

everything.com sells its big search division to IBM

Chuck Newberg, CEO, announced IBM had bought everything.com's fast growing search division for $5 billion in cash, would move the headquarters to Tucson, and everything.com would use the proceeds to buyback their stock immediately. IBM used JP Morgan as their advisers and everything.com the Sloan.

Joyce called George at 7 AM that morning with the news. George paused, "They do move fast and yes, you were right, they are a mobile force. Thatcher was extremely circumspect on the phone about everything.com. The bad news is they are a mobile force; the good news is Thatcher is on the inside."

"George, I think we should consider canceling our meeting this morning with the Commissioner about our progress, or lack of it, and get over there before there is no there there."

"Quite a sentence, Joyce."

"Yes, and?"

"And I want to keep my job. I'm not going to be the one to tell the Commissioner someone is more important in our police work than he is; and I won't have you doing it either, or you will be Iphigenia on the funeral pyre courtesy of our Agamemnon, the Commissioner."

"Your reading sometimes surprises me, George."

"Good; gotta keep my sneaky slider for days like this when I suspect I will need it. This is getting worse and worse. I'll bet we get blamed for the move."

At 11 AM they did. The Commissioner was upset by no progress, the Mayor was asking him about driving everything.com out of New York, and the list of their sins went on from there. When George suggested that next they'll think he did the murder, the Commissioner said, possibly, but I think you'll get a pass on that one. And he said it with no humor. So things weren't good when they left, had lunch, and walked over to everything.com.

When they walked in and showed their credentials to Security on the ground floor, they were told everything.com had moved to Tucson.

"I want to see Jim Johnson," George said acerbically, having a continuing bad day."

"Sir, I am sorry to have been unclear. They have moved to Tucson."

"Certainly not yet; I just want to see him, or at least talk to him."

"Sir, they have moved. Their two floors are closed off until the tenants above them move down to fill up the space, which they are in the process of doing now as we speak."

"Tenants above them?"

"Yes, Bank of America, sir. They have been looking to expand and this was a great opportunity for them." George knew a sporting fish on the run or swim as it were, and let him do just that until he wound down about the many virtues of BOA.

George got even by saying, "They must tip well?"

The man grinned and that told the story. But that didn't help much with his problem. It did make George feel better and that was not unimportant at the low tide he was now at. So that was something with the slim pickings so far today.

"OK, do they have anyone on the premises or do you have a forwarding address?"

"Two no's sir, I am sorry. Nothing. In fact, to be honest, no one told me anything other than BOA was moving down, the floors were closed off, and I was to tell people that if asked. Which I have, haven't I?"

George ignored that, and said, "What about your rental office, would they know more?"

"I doubt it sir. Even I know that BOA was looking for more space and said they would jump at any opening; this worked out well being right above everything. I'll bet they did it on a phone call between the principals to save money."

The Security Man would be right. When George finally got a hold of the BOA office manager he confirmed those facts. "Yes, we just got the word early this morning and we are so excited. My bosses in Charlotte were pushing us and we finally delivered. A big relief, I'll tell you. Who? Jim Johnson their CFO. Where did he go? I don't know a Jim Johnson. everything.com signed the paperwork though. All legal and simple, which things can be when the lawyers don't get in it to run up their legal hours and the fees. Heck, we are moving in right now as we speak."

The term "as we speak" was getting on George's nerves. George asked about everything moving their things.

"Inspector, this is the cyber age; now I am not as up to date with it as I should be but what was there to move? We are just

55

taking over their desks, basic computer equipment, and everything else. You know, someone from everything told me they had done the same thing with the previous tenant."

"Our head office in Charlotte was darn pleased I am told. So we will have part of the office up and running later today. Pretty cool. No New York unions to hassle with about moving stuff, arguing, paying, bribing, etc. and so forth since they don't even know it happened and, even if they did, couldn't get by security downstairs. Heck you know all about that as an Inspector." He stopped and George nodded so he would go on.

"Well can you at least let me walk through?"

"Sure, delighted. Nice talking to someone who knows all about this."

Joyce was about to interrupt, but George waved her off. Better he think they weren't total fools or he might clam up then. But, on the other hand, the guy seemed to like to yack. That never hurt but he would have to see whether it helped.

They took the elevator down from the BOA's man's office. The BOA man indicated they would start on the bottom floor and then move up to the second one when George was ready to do so. George nodded his agreement.

The elevator opened to the former everything.com lobby Johnson had talked to them in. There were no changes he noticed; for the first time he realized there had not been a corporate insignia when he visited before. He asked Joyce, "Do you remember any corporate signs out here yesterday?"

"No. And I thought it was odd then. It looks just the same now. Do you remember we had to buzz in on that speaker over there? We only saw a man who said he was Johnson and gave us a general address card. Didn't have any person's name on it." Were they being paranoid? She wondered.

George described the man and the BOA office manager shook his head saying, "Never met any executive like that from everything. There was a private investigator they used that fit that description. As I recall he had been a real cowboy and they hired him because he was used to being quiet, or that's what I was told about him. Maybe that was an urban legend. But it seemed right. I can't exactly remember his name; but it wasn't Jim or Johnson as I recall."

That explained it George thought. The everything man had been calm, respectful, and aloof; definitely not characteristics associated with rambunctious New Yorkers always thinking they had to push back to create a little space for themselves in the maelstrom of city life. George had learned this from police conferences when the small city guys were more like the everything.com PI.

They just didn't have to fight for space because there was a lot of it, perhaps too much for many of them. Well he had sure been fooled much like in Mark Twain's *The Jumping Frog of Calaveras County*, who turned out couldn't jump due to buck shot put in his belly. Well, this guy certainly tricked them without any buckshot required, just pure BS, and not much of that, which had been the persuader.

With those thoughts, they were walking through a sea of standard office equipment. He asked Joyce, "Tell me what you see." The BOA Man looked at him quizzically but Joyce knew what he meant so did so as she made notes on her iPhone at the same time.

Then she started giving George the running commentary he liked. "First, no file cabinets; second desks or rather tables without drawers; third few waste baskets, printers, or similar things. As a result, a lot more table and chair space for people; I'll bet they had about twice the number of people that these offices used to have. And open lighting because of no private offices around the edges."

The BOA man pitched in. "Yes, our people are following this layout. They think they will be able to comfortably put twice the number of people here we usually get into this size space. They aren't going to build out private offices; the mucky mucks will keep theirs in our executive area 3 floors up."

They moved into the amenities area. "George," Joyce continued, "they have devoted a lot of space to people taking a bit of time from their desks or should I say tables? Great food equipment; massage chairs; exercise room; lounge; no reason for them to leave the floor at lunch or at other times during the day for that matter. Private lockers too. Handy for deliveries from Amazon and others as well as to safely store your own stuff."

The BAO man said, "Yes, and shorter hours and more work. Our bosses liked the way they ran it. They tried to get everyone to leave their desks, or should I say tables too, by 5 PM. Sometimes they partied in the lounge; sometimes they moved out. But they were among the first to leave the building. They picked up a number of our employees for that reason. Nice folks; easy going; no execs and slaves, so to speak. I liked them too," which said a lot George thought. No one seemed to have an axe to grind about everything.com. Usually Security people and office managers like the BOA guy did. But not this time, not with this crew. An informant would be hard to find, what this Police specialist was looking for, and he'd been cut off by a real honest to goodness cowboy. These guys are good, he concluded.

On the next floor, Joyce got it and said so. "George, what I see is a fancy college dorm or frat layout. Everything you wanted: relaxed work, collegiality, free everything since there are no vending machines, and short work hours. Yep, a frat on steroids."

The BOA man heard this with approval. "Yes, Miss. Exactly. I hadn't seen it that clearly. They had a college enthusiasm about them. Nice to see. Good of the company to maintain. They

58

recycled everything. The maintenance staff said there was little to maintain. I asked one of them once about that. He said in cyberspace you don't need physical objects like printers, paper, file cabinets, and all the things that result in waste and mess. He said they generally ate fresh things, so composting was easy too. No potato chips for them!"

All of this applause would make things harder. Much harder, George knew from experience, as if things weren't hard enough already.

They took another tour of the 2 floors to see if they picked up any new data. They didn't. But a thought flashed across Joyce's face, so George asked, "What?"

"Is the crime scene done and removed?"

"Yes. As you know with important people we get a lot of pressure to do so, especially from neighbors and others that have influence and clout. What?" as he saw her shake her head.

"George, we have been a step or two behind these people at every pass. That cowboy was a fake. That wasn't an accident; we didn't notice any nervousness by him in his silence. How were we to know? He spoke with a flat Iowa accent. You call Thatcher, of the Sloan, and he says fine, tomorrow at 5 PM. Well, according to *The Journal* the company was sold and that publicly announced before then. Its move was announced. So your Thatcher broke no confidences. Good for him; bad for us." And she paused as George tried to get his bearings on this one.

"Then, George, we twig onto, 'hey, they'll be gone soon,' and when we arrive to check that out we find the whole kit and caboodle is gone; the place swept clean, who knows maybe fingerprint clean; and someone else has already started moving in. We couldn't stop them if we tried; and if we did, what would we find, just this," as she pointed to an unoccupied sea of office equipment. Well, not exactly she thought; because when she turned around she saw the first new BOA people moving in.

59

"We go back downstairs and a whole bunch of BOA people have moved in with their badges, coats and ties, and lovely dresses. Wait, I hear an elevator unloading and more voices there." She paused, "Yep they are invading their own space now," as she shook her head.

"Has it occurred to you what has to me?"

"What? They, whoever they is, got the victim's place cleaned spic and span other than the actual crime scene, right?" George nodded. "Well, they undoubtedly know the crime scene was taken down. Right?" George nodded again; he was staggered by the speed of it all. "They rerented this place with a business to business agreement, no lawyers, so it was fast and simple."

"We haven't seen the document but what do you bet it is one of those electronic signature things, which means Newberg could have signed it anywhere in the world and forwarded it on."

George nodded again but thought, hey this is so fast and ugly, and Joyce and I may even miss the blame. He grimaced, no. Someone will have to take it and who better than us? A just the facts set of reports was called for. He was glad he had watched the old Jack Webb *Dragnet* TV shows. Webb got it right.

George noticed Joyce was waiting for him to catch up, or at least get closer. He nodded and she went on, "I'll bet they have already sold those two condos and someone else is moving in now, right now. Trophy space. Used to be crime scenes brought the value down; now it is modern theater, bizarre, but we know it is true." George thought he was going to get sick.

"What do we do, Joyce?"

"We leave here and walk back there and see what is what. They walked back to the condos. When they entered the lobby there was a new Security Guard and a Big Shot boss type backing him up. When they checked in, the Security Guard handed him a document headed:

The crime scene is closed. All information is available to those authorized at Centre Street New York Police Headquarters, at the Commissioner's Office.

"So we would still like to see the property."

"Sir, it has been sold and they are moving in now, well they are redoing the place actually."

"What about the old furniture?"

"I don't know sir; they used the service elevator and took what they took. They have full authorization."

Here the Big Boss inserted himself, "Hello, I am Hal Williams. I am the General Foreman for the new owners that wish to remain anonymous and, of course, they never were here when the sad event took place and did not know the victim."

"How did the sale take place, Hal?" From experience he knew that would jar Williams and it did, but only ever so slightly. Hal waited and righted himself before speaking. A wise habit George thought as he waited.

"I am authorized to give you this, Inspector," as he handed him a document.

The Olson Family Trust Buys the Everything Condos

Today the Trust announced they had bought the 2 founders of everything.com's condos in a private transaction.

"That's it?"

"That's it, Sir. They asked me to wait for you in the lobby should you have any further questions."

"I have a 1000 questions. Who do I talk to about them?" George was heated up and Joyce gave him the high sign to mellow out. "Hal, I know you are working on instructions but what would you recommend?" This was a hard one to field. Hal paused for quite a long time.

"I don't know, Inspector. I have no instructions as to that."

George looked at him menacing, but that cut no ice with Hal. George concluded Hal was probably a bouncer or had been. He would bet he was no more a foreman than he was. But, they had set this up well so he asked for his name and contact information.

Hal was clearly prepared for this and handed him a general company card, with no specific name on it. George thought back to police school. They had been told the toughest witnesses were those who didn't give an inch and stonewalled you from hello. Even worse were situations, rare ones, where everyone around the perpetrator did this. Well, he had gotten that treatment so far. No one had moved an inch and that wasn't by accident. Planning had gone into this. Impromptu perhaps; but planning nevertheless.

He took a chance, "Hal, do you have a personal card?"

"No."

"Then show me some ID."

"You don't have reasonable cause, sir."

Yep, a bouncer. He knew the rules. Tough guy. Well a tough guy for sure. He took a last shot.

"How do I even know you are Hal Williams?"

Hal just looked at him with no expression, backed up, pushed the elevator button, and was gone.

George turned to the Security Man and said, "I want to go up."

"I am not authorized to permit that, sir. Anyway they have turned off the floor for the elevator so that won't work; the stairs doors work by code on the outside and I don't even have it; inside they open smoothly as tested by your fire department so they pass code."

George looked at him, "Your fire department?" Who was this guy?

George followed on with, "Do you have some ID?

"You don't have reasonable cause, sir."

What got George is neither one had made any snarky comments. They were totally trained, almost military trained. Well, perhaps they had been; nothing would surprise him now.

As a parting shot he said, "We will be back."

The Security Man didn't even nod.

As they left, George was mumbling curses. Joyce said, "Let's hit that pub again. You need it," and smiled, and her smile lit up the world, especially after all those dark clouds today.

He nodded as they moved off. "We have to walk a bit first, Joyce. I have some thinking to do."

"I don't have a punching bag for you so the walk, beer, and burger are the best we can do for you," as she gave him a friendly nudge.

"Well what do you think Joyce? You got to see it, live and in color."

Joyce said quietly: "My bets have been good so far. Our next step is to come back after lunch. I'll lay you odds neither guy will be there. It is like we put our finger in a glass of water, pull it out, and there is no trace. These guys are good, check that. They are great. There are great brains behind all this. It must be Chuck since Jack is dead. He is dead for sure isn't he?"

He almost rose to the bait but saw her grin and just broke into convulsive laughter with her. They needed that. They had been making the bumbling 1969 Mets look like a winning team.

Chapter 12

John Putnam Thatcher

He has a 41" reach so I'll stay at 42

Back at the Pub the owner came over and said, "You guys look like you had a hard day."

"Tell me about it," and they shared some Irish stories, gossip, and generally had a good time. Joyce kept nodding at the owner to fill George's glass. George wasn't against the idea. When 2 hours passed, they went back. Yep, 2 new guys.

George said, "Let's call it a day. I'll see you at the Devonshire tomorrow at 5 PM to meet with Thatcher. Take the rest of today and tomorrow off until then. Clear the pipes; get ready for a truly informative experience after all this oppositional nonsense, but rather I should say, expertise.

Joyce raised an eyebrow, "But you know how important it is to get things fast; a few days and everything evaporates."

"Yes, and they know that," as she nodded. "They have outfoxed and outgunned us. Best information so far is from *The Journal*, as you call it familiarly. We will see what it brings tomorrow."

The next day's headline was instructive:

everything.com announced an LBO

Elizabeth Thatcher, SVP of the Sloan, announced Chuck Newberg, CEO of everything.com, succeeded in getting 91% of its stock for cash in an LBO, using cash from the sale to IBM and its own funds to do so. "The investors benefited from liquefying their position before the stock dropped further and the company benefits from being able to transform itself from a high growth to steady EPS firm at a lower marketcap." She concluded by saying, "The speed of the sale to IBM and LBO speaks to the value the outsiders got."

So their number one suspect now owned effectively the whole company. Yes, his 26% before was worth more; but minority stakes in companies weren't as valuable as majority ownership, even at lower prices he knew. Further, the Sloan itself had done a similar thing to escape US taxes and control, plus do an LBO to escape SEC and public scrutiny as well. Chuck couldn't have used a more seasoned group than the largest bank in the world, the Sloan.

Proof was another thing. George was getting a feel for Chuck. Chuck knew how to give up space for time, rather like Stalin did with Hitler in World War II. That took longer than this. Chuck had aced the test. Chuck wasted no time or effort to indicate it wasn't him; none at all. He just covered his tracks and vamoosed somewhere. They didn't even know where or if they were ever going to be able to talk to him again.

The fast evacuations meant Chuck was taking no chances on physical evidence, interrogations, and the like. Selling and moving the company helped achieve that purpose. And it wasn't just a move down the road to White Plains like Pepsi did when moving out of the City.

George went to wsj.com to see if there were other announcements relating to this. There were:

SEC announced everything.com was delisted on NASDAQ

The SEC announced today that the company did not have sufficient float or number of stockholders to be on NASDAQ any longer. The shares would sell on pink sheets until the final percentages were bought in their LBO.

Everything.com announces 98% of the stock has been
acquired.
The Sloan announced 98% had now been acquired. The rest
would be acquired by routine, their spokesperson reported

George kept puzzling over Joyce's term, a mobile force. Yes they were. Cyber companies were no longer tied down to a physical place pounding out widgets or selling food. Now they could move and escape from government and agency oversight that relied on physical locations to inspect factories, offices, stores, and the like, and frankly nail them. In other words, to enforce their edicts. No more.

What was there to inspect at the old everything.com office or even at the owners' condos? They were clearly transitory and easily left behind. Even disposing of them was much simpler as the rich had far more cash, as did companies, compared to his youth when big companies had tons of debt and moved at a lumbering pace. The people of course. In the old days, the people couldn't escape questions they did not want to answer, whether guilty or innocent. Now they were able to escape oversight and investigation more easily since their assets weren't as predominantly physical, tied to physical locations.

Now the everything.com people didn't have to worry so much about interrogation because they had crossed state lines and were not subject to questioning by federal agencies since it was a local crime in New York, 2000 miles from Arizona where most now were.

Now these successful modern companies also had tons of cash. Debt used to tie them down somewhat too; but these companies don't have much or any debt anymore since equity fueled companies these days with an abundance of cash available in the investment world. It was something indeed, that George was now experiencing first hand. Well, John Putnam Thatcher, he thought, was his last best chance. He would be right about that.

At 5 PM he arrived at the Devonshire where Joyce was waiting for him. She had gotten dressed up in an outfit similar to those George had seen on society women, subtle, elegant, and appropriate. This would help since George always looked like what he was, an Inspector, despite the best of suits, one of which he had on at the moment.

They were announced in and went up the elevator to John's. He greeted them at the door in casual elegant clothes that reminded George of pictures of gentlemen on Nantucket. Well, John was a gentleman and would fit right in on that elegant island northeast of them where the nobs hung out during the summers. Well, George thought, Thatcher was a nob after all.

A somewhat elderly but handsome servant guided the 3 of them into John's living room which had a full bar and Hors d'oeuvres out. They looked good. Even if they were there on grim business it would be a lovely evening George was sure. He would be right.

John opened up the conversation. "Nice to see you, George, and your young lady too," nodding towards her in a grandfatherly way. He continued, "Why don't I tell you what I know and see if that works for you. My daughter, Elizabeth, can tell you more. As if on cue, and probably was, a 35 to 40 year old woman appeared who was evidently the SVP of the Sloan now headquartered in Dublin.

She had clearly downplayed her appearance in order to fit in and not appear too attractive, aggressive or uncordial. It was a good effort but she was too attractive and intelligent looking to pull it off. No, it wasn't quite that George surmised. She was too shrewd and agile, like her father, to quite pull that off.

She was in street talk, a sharp cookie, and that was that. He noticed that she had let Joyce and him appraise her without pressure. She had not pushed the conversation. She was there to support it; but, he suspected, it was the Sloan first as with him it was the New York City Police first. The sides were established. They could now move forward he thought.

"Yes, sir, John. Why don't you proceed and see where it takes us."

John nodded and launched in as Albert Nelson started serving the drinks. "First, I thought you would like to know more about our cast of characters,. Albert Nelson, who is serving the drinks, started with me at the Sloan 20 years or so ago."

"Miss Corsa, my secretary who you have met, used Albert for a number of tasks on my behalf as well as the Sloan in general. It was a few years before I learned how helpful he was, how he had tuned into me, and how things worked out when Albert was involved," as the two of them exchanged glances and smiled at each other.

"Then I moved up to Chairman, which meant overseeing not running around as I used to do. Unlike Lancer, I had no interest in writing for *Foreign Affairs*, or traveling hither yither and yon like Withers, so I have stayed more personally involved in our business."

"Albert essentially runs the personal condos for the Sloan here on the 6th and 7th floors. He lives in my mother-in-law apartment because there is only me here now. Elizabeth has her own place on the floor above. Jack has his elsewhere. My daughter Laura, her husband and family, are happily located in the suburbs. And my other son is well situated elsewhere and stays with Elizabeth when visiting New York."

"Why is this important? It provides a glimpse into a 2 man relationship at work and play, as Jack and Chuck had. Ours is clearer: I have the boss role and Albert the subordinate one. We have become closer over the years but nothing has fundamentally changed."

"My relationship with my college roommate, Tom Robichaux, has lasted 50 years despite all the goings on in our lives. My son Jack joined his firm and is now a partner and, like Elizabeth at the Sloan, set to take over when Tom and Devane decide to retire. Neither has any children so that makes it peaceful."

"I have never had a balanced 2 man relationship as Chuck and Jack had. Those are hard from what I know of them. When we invest we want tandems like that to decide who is in charge. That often wrecks the deal, but anything else has been proven not to work. So Jack was the nominal CEO and Chuck the COO, technically reporting to him despite them owning equal amounts of stock and having a buy sell agreement between them."

"In the Wall Street world status comes from your pile of cash and position; Jack had both; Chuck had the former but not the latter. There are those who would snicker at that situation Chuck was put in. And that is never pleasant. So I think you should start there."

"Now let's have another drink, dinner, and we can talk some more. I think it best if Elizabeth carry the ball now about the recent goings on."

And   that   was   that   until   later.

Chapter 13

Elizabeth Thatcher

You drive for show but putt for dough

They had had a nice dinner as Joyce and Elizabeth got to know each other and John, Albert, and George shared stories and wine together. Albert set a good table and everyone pitched in to help with the serving. It was a pleasant time for Elizabeth and John, but a uniquely nice one for Joyce and George. Albert loved presiding over such events so was beaming through the meal.

Elizabeth started out. "The Sloan was involved with the Company pretty much from hello. The boys as I always call them, roomed together at Harvard and HBS, and seemed to be as close as people get. They liked the same things, but had complementing talents so did not interfere with each other. Rather like a baseball team. We like companies that have spread out the infield, with not everyone at first or third, like just engineers on one corner or sales people on the other.

"Jack was the rainmaker; Chuck carried the water, as he used to say. It was a dot.com hype sales company so Jack was the front man and thus CEO to make deals. Chuck got things done, kept expenses down, and was immensely practical."

"They had no issues in their early struggles. As John says, as I call him in business, entrepreneurs remember the hard days when they struggle to pay their bills. When they can pay them, they often get bored, nervous, and worse. Bankers like us, of course, are the opposite. We invest to get them over that hump so paying the bills, including our loans, is merely routine."

"About 3 years ago they got over the hump. They had an IPO with a $2 billion market cap, big for those days. Jack did all kinds of things to boost their market cap to $16 billion, but then the partners started to have some issues, which I noticed."

"We had provided their first $2 million in equity capital quite a while before their IPO. We got repaid in about 24 months which meant our equity kicker was knocked back to 5% from 10%. If they had taken 5 years to repay it would have been 20% and up from there. Chuck promised we would get paid quickly and he delivered. As far as we were concerned, better 5% of a going cash flowing concern than 20% or more of a problem one."

"Frankly, we never liked the business and didn't really trust Jack, the rainmaker. So we dealt with Chuck. We had a board seat until the loan was repaid. Once repaid we went off the board which was just as well for us, cutting down our fiduciary duties, and therefore our risk being on a soon to be public board."

"We received another 3% of the stock for arranging the IPO plus our fees. In any event, we quickly placed about $1.5 billion with a few major funds. $250 million with smaller funds. And the remaining $250 million with our best individual customers and trusts that wanted in. At the IPO we sold our 5% kicker from the initial loan and received $100 million for that alone."

"I set a hard ceiling of $10 billion at which point all individual customers and our 3% would be sold off. I sold 1% at $5 billion and we got $50 million on that. And then the other 2% at $10 billion so got $200 million for that tranche, quite a nice little profit with no fuss or muss."

"The trust department was supposed to sell off the remainder for its clients. We had made them pledge to do so if we allocated stock to them. We encouraged the early funds to do likewise. As the Swiss say, you can't get hurt taking a profit.

But this was more than a little. At $10 billion it was a 5 to 1 return and they reached it in just 24 months."

"Most sold; some of our individual customers refused to do so. We had made them sign hold harmless releases if they wanted to break their written agreement with us to sell at $10 billion market cap. Yes, George?"

"Wasn't that tough, Elizabeth? I mean tough terms?"

"Yes and no, as with most things," as she smiled at him. "Yes it was tough because we were enforcing an agreement we had forced upon them to receive their allocation of shares; no because Wall Street is full of litigation about you should have told me, you should have forced me to get out, etc. and so on."

"And what do we do? Settle. So we lose. It is only a question of how much we lose. So no, it was not tough to enforce that written provision. We still got some mad people when the stock crashed to $6 billion the other day, and then went lower on the buyout news. Darn mad people because remember, just a few days earlier it was at $20 billion and they believed they did it themselves by disregarding our agreement. When it crashed it became our fault for not enforcing the agreements. It never is money until you sell, but most people overlook that fact."

"So how big is the collective investment of your accounts in the Company?" Joyce asked.

"In their minds about $1 billion based on the $20 billion valuation; $500 million on the $10 billion cap; and $250 million on the LBO at $5 billion, which is a fairly private number and I hope you will try to keep it that way."

George and Joyce nodded. They were aware Elizabeth had been forthright and used subtle nudge words and phrases such as "fairly" private and "I hope you will try to keep it that way." George thought people he interrogated could learn from that.

Well, who couldn't learn from a Thatcher, he thought? About no one was the answer.

She was definitely a chip off the old block and clearly positioned well in the cyberworld where you can be anywhere in the world, even a bank which most of us think of as a bunch of buildings, he reflected. But they weren't and that was the point; the buildings were like a Hollywood set as where their vaults were for show, not where the money was or ever had been.

Of course, the importance of anywhere in the world was they could move easily and seamlessly, just like everything.com did, at the first hint of trouble, to sidestep litigation, government inquiry, or any other troubling local matters. At the first beating of the tom toms as he thought of it. Clearly businesses had seized control from governments. For example, even Heinz was selling more American ketchup worldwide than in the US as stated in their last SEC report. And CEOs talk to each other; the tipping point had or would be reached shortly. Companies of all types were becoming the mobile forces Joyce described.

Elizabeth would be tuned into the issue. Possibly even hardwired into it. But, as with all good investigators, he did not interrupt forthcoming witnesses so let her go on with her story rather than interrupt it with his new questions. They could wait and, possibly, many would be answered in her narrative without asking at all. He would be right.

"As Uncle Everett says, few people can read a balance sheet and it takes that to understand this." George couldn't believe anyone could call Everett Gabbler, that frosty hardcore pessimist, Uncle, and do so with warmth. This girl, ah woman he corrected himself, had possibilities. He could call men boys, as long as they were white he corrected himself, but never women girls, no matter the race, creed, or color. It was tough living up to these modern PC standards he mused, as Elizabeth continued.

"George, Everett says you can, which is a rare compliment from him." Well she knew the crusty old foggy. Not fooled by his mild look at this statement, she almost winked at him as she saw those thoughts go through his mind. She was fun too. If he had been 25 years younger, richer, more handsome, and better educated, he would love to try for her. He started giggling. He couldn't help it. She gave him a look and a wink, indicating she probably knew what he was thinking. Clairvoyant too, he mused. John and Albert had seen this before but Joyce was baffled. Understandably so.

Elizabeth continued. "OK, let's go through the numbers. First, as John said, these guys measure how big they are by their pile of cash and position."

At this point Joyce interjected, "I think it takes a girl to say it, but it's like those Oxford boys who have a pecking order based on who can pee farthest in the snow," and Elizabeth joined her in a chuckle, gave her Dad a wink, and they all broke out in laughter. Good they all thought. Nice to lighten up the atmosphere.

Albert, being no fool, poured everyone another drink. The party was moving right along with their own little soap opera.

"So Chuck pushed for the Simply acquisition because they had $100 million pretax profit and free cashflow on just over $110 million in sales, no small feat. They were growing 20% per year without great effort; they were price and quality leaders in the untapped audiobook market and well positioned in the much larger eBook market."

"Chuck had his favorite, but considered boring, division earning $500 million pretax, growing at 12% per year. So combining just those 2 would give him $600 million pretax; since he had positioned both in Ireland with only their 12.5% tax rate, and being all cyber that was pretty easy to do, that would be $500 million per year in after tax earnings. All he had to do was sell the rest off, and that was the sexy business that people wanted

75

in on, especially IBM, a laggard compared to the fast moving Amazons and others. So he did."

"The problem for bragging rights on the Street was these divisions together did only $900 million in sales, a lousy top line number. But, and this is a gigantic but, no working capital was involved since these 2 remaining divisions only have $300 million in annual expenses of the $900 million total sales, most of which expenses are only due a few days after receipt of customer payments."

"Sounds like your own little ATM," George said with a whistle.

"Yes. But Chuck knew that Jack would have nothing to do with that approach. Chuck told me he had broached it. Clearly the pee in the snow thing, as Joyce said," and they smiled in unison. "So that's why Chuck is my prime candidate for you. Now let's talk about the personal impact of these numbers for Chuck."

"Conventional wisdom says Chuck was better off with Jack alive. He would have 26% of $20 billion or over $5 billion in the Company. With Jack dead he had 26% of a $5 billion company or just over $1 billion; even with Jack's share under their buy/sell agreement he had only $2 billion in equity, or less than 40% of what he had when Jack was alive."

"But Chuck knew it was an increasingly teetering enterprise that would collapse if the momentum or other trends went against them since they had no earnings due to the sales for sales sake division with substantial losses. In addition, Chuck clearly believed Jack would keep doubling down like some drunk casino player until he lost it all. In short, there would be no payout for Chuck and lots of sweat trying to keep everything going. Chuck once told me a telling story, 'You can juggle the eggs expertly; but sooner or later they hit you in the head.'"

"Chuck knew how to fix everything.com in the 'drive for show but putt for dough' strategy that the short game of nickels dimes and quarters is how you win, something Simply and the remaining division have been masterful at."

"Accordingly, the moment he could, Chuck sold off the fancy profitless cash draining division to IBM, which IBM had been set up to do quietly for some time now through our efforts at the Sloan. I doubt Jack even knew about it. And, and this is a big and, remember all the expensive people and overhead went with that division to Tucson. In short, Chuck created a situation where he never had to see them again and doubt he will do so voluntarily. My hunch, but like John, I am a hunch player."

She continued with a slight grin, "Chuck has a grind it out dot.com left, that is an automated fully functional B2C business in a few basic niches that require no fancy dancers, equipment, or locations."

"The Simply business is a pure download one unless a physical retailer wants to put up a hard net 30 day PO and take delivery from a third party manufacturer. No warehouse, no shipping, no fuss, no muss for Simply in that scenario either."

"OK. We have the picture," Joyce said.

"Translate to my little world, Elizabeth," George added.

"OK. On the face of it Chuck had a mess on his hands with the large sexy teetering division. But, and this is a big but, he could drive the train once Jack was gone. Chuck knew which track to go on."

"IBM had been talking to us as I just said; we had floated the idea to Chuck; all he really had to do was say yes and it was done, as it was. Chuck got us to prepare an agreement, as he always did, before even looking at the deal. This saved a lot of time and was a great idea. We have since adopted this practice widely by having an agreed upon document with only the purchase price to be filled in by the parties; no other negotiations permitted. Clients who use this process benefit;

77

those that don't are often like Indians paddling towards the sunset. They keep paddling and the sun keeps still being out there."

They nodded as if in a chorus. They were on board with her description and concepts.

"It was a simple no warranty no guarantee deal. $5 billion bought IBM everything on a purchase order. No stock, no notes, no AR, no AP, no bills, no real estate, no employees or anything else to audit or mull over. Whatever they did about all that was up to them separately. IBM quickly recruited everyone. I think everyone signed on but a few clericals. Tucson is a nice place, cheap, and IBM maintained their New York City salary levels so it was a big pay raise for all of them that joined IBM there. IBM also paid for all moving expenses and temporary quarters out there until they were each fully settled."

"The Sloan got the IBM money; used it to fund the purchase of the outstanding everything.com stock. We got to 91% based on several calls and 98% today. The rest we can force through in what is called a cram down. Simple and legal. As Chuck said, the worst that happens is we pay the holdouts a little more. Since it is only 1.5% now at last count, as even 25% of the remaining 2% drifted in, that means we expect to get that below 1% of the total stock within a week. If we even doubled the payout to those left, that would only be another 1%. So the stock crash worked wonders for Chuck."

"Tell us a bit more, if you would," Joyce added.

"OK. Let me put it in sports terms. You have 3 professional teams. One churns out a lot of cash with good upside, but is a low minor league team like Elmira for the Red Sox. That's Simply. One is solid but still just a minor league team in Triple A, like Pawtucket, and the remaining everything.com division. The third is a famous major league franchise but a perennial money loser, like the division the company sold off to IBM. So

Chuck is left with two productive minor league teams, and that is where major league talent comes from, after all. Just need a bit of patience to see who turns into a really good hitter, to extend the analogy. So the true upside is with the 2 minor league teams or the remaining 2 divisions Chuck now owns lock, stock, and barrel."

"Ah, I really get it now," said George. "Those minor leaguers really love the game; they aren't spoiled; they just want a crack at the big time. Most just enjoy another year in the sun playing ball and getting paid. Yes, less stress, more cash, less envy, simpler life, and more growth potential. After all, once in the majors where is there to go?"

"And importantly, George, something Chuck does well."

"Now there is a point, a darn good one. Now tell me about this automatic pilot ATM company. Roughly how many people, how many locations, how much to do, how much to change, etc.

"Let's build from the foundation up rather than from 40,000 feet down. Simply has about 1100 downloadable titles. That works out to about 50,000 per title sold worldwide at their net receipts of about $2 per title, some more some less or $100,000 each. On their own site they get more, about $4 per title; they prefer to sell through others but $4 is a pretty good number too. 50,000 copies of each title is not a huge hurdle to achieve. A very Elmira kind of activity, with 4,000 fans a good turnout versus needing 40,000 in the majors."

"These are evergreen backlist audiobook and eBook titles that do not require updating like software. The titles either are on their relatively cheap $1000 per month server or on their distributor or customer servers at no cost to Simply. They have never had a title discontinued. There is no shelfspace issue in cyberspace so maintaining listings for them is no big deal and therefore requires no sales staff."

"They use a few contractors to maintain their server at very minimum expense because the server company, IBM in fact through another division, does most of that as part of their service. Updating new titles is a relatively simple straightforward process too. They have no invoicing; their accounts ACH wire all payments to their Sloan checking account so no accounting staff is required. The former principal developed or wrote most of the about 50 new titles per year, which is only about 1 per week, so there is no heavy lifting involved. Simply had and required no office, factory, warehouse, or other physical facility. Their expenses are primarily limited to authors they have permanent imperpetuity agreements with that they pay out on. Most are free to Simply forever contracts. Those authors get bragging rights for consulting gigs, employment benefits, or just personal pleasure. Sometimes all 3. The few paid authors get a money split after ACH funds are received, with no guarantees, minimums or audit rights. All on the same sweet one page agreement."

"Simple like their name."

"Exactly. The other division, the everything.com one, operates much the same way but has various niches that require more TLC. They too have automated most functions. They have a swat team staff of about 20 contractors, but no employees. So you have a $900 million company with no W2's, physical facilities or equipment, and none of the employee and physical issues and risks that go with those things. Sweet, no?"

"Right up Chuck's alley, I can tell from knowing him. Nirvana for him; would be hell for Jack. We know all this because we do all everything.com's banking for free, using some of the float to give us our fees. We do the accounting, tax filing, payments to authors, and more. Chuck encourages our belt and suspenders conservative approach to accounting and tax payments, which leads governments and agencies to know that if anything they are getting more than their due. All good for everyone involved: Simply, the remaining division, the Sloan, and the tax agencies."

"So let's see if I have this right," said George. "This guy Chuck now has a $900 million company with no debt, right?" and Elizabeth nodded. "It delivers $10 million after tax profit every week?" and she nodded again. "But he has no public stock value and the company isn't very sexy without the big time division IBM bought," and she nodded again. "So what could he get for it?"

"Normally these kinds of niche players get 7x to 10x of their cashflow or profits. That means $3.5 to $5 billion. But, in this case, with the ATM feature, it could go higher. And another but. If Chuck does his thing, with the brand name and more, he can grow the business substantially without having to imagine or invent anything new. Note that he couldn't have done that with Jack because Chuck would constantly have to fix, repair, triage, and more the big division. Now he can concentrate on the ATM that works, like *The Little Engine that Could*," and she smiled.

"In sum, that gives him motive, opportunity, and means. We have just 2 problems; we have no proof and we can't find him," George said.

"Yes," John said. "And you can see he has no reason to be found. I suggest we adjourn the discussion on this basis keeping in mind that he is the most probable perpetrator but you need to focus most now on finding him, as you know. After that other things can follow. So come back tomorrow at 5 PM, and we will do round 2?"

"Wonderful," Joyce said. "We can enjoy looking forward to that too, as we did tonight. George, we can report in we are still working the problem without disclosing the confidential information we have gratefully received," and left them with a smile.

They chatted amiably for half an hour or so before George and Joyce left.

When they did so, Albert and Elizabeth turned to John for his appraisal and summing up.

"The story points to Chuck. What I see from my perspective is Chuck may well have wanted a rest. Jack wouldn't have given him that. Jack, like Alexander the Great, wanted to take the next hill, the next province, the next country. When his men found out that was his plan, they rebelled; and Alexander died on the way home because he couldn't stop from fighting. They had all the booty they required long before they started back to Greece, but the habit was too deep."

"That's the way I see it here. Chuck rebelled; didn't talk about it because he knew Jack too well. No point in that. It would just lead to Chuck getting whacked somehow."

"This way Chuck avoided dealing with Jack again. Chuck was tired of playing wet nurse to the messy division; so he dumped that too; he was tired of the fancy dancers and fancy dancing so he sent them to IBM; he was tired of the office and closed it; he was tired of the condos so sold them."

"He has skillfully made the Sloan responsible for all government reporting and tax payments. As the largest bank in the world, and a private one now thanks to Elizabeth and our team, we need make no SEC disclosures of any of this. He has set up a pass through tax situation so his personal taxes are paid before we disburse any money to him. So he is getting 100% clean funds, certified by us and any government authorities that get involved. He authorized a legal fund to deal with any of it but I doubt if that will be necessary because he does not want any tax advantaged anything."

"Elizabeth, what has he instructed you with regard to disbursements going forward?"

"He asked that we make available to him $1 million in cash in each of his Toronto, New York, London, Paris, Bonn, Geneva, and Athens correspondent bank safe deposit boxes. After that he said to put the proceeds equally into Apple, Amazon, and Dollar Tree stocks until we are notified further. He asked to be included in any major VC commitments available that we approve of and has authorized me to invest up to $10 million on his behalf in any one of my choosing without consulting him. He's like that. Easy to deal with."

John interrupted, "You know what I think? I think we should buy some Amazon, Apple, and Dollar Tree based on his getting everything else right." He chuckled; Albert took note. He would do exactly that. Albert knew how to avoid getting trapped by inside information; this was just John's opinion, albeit a skilled professional. A little tricky because of the data from Elizabeth, but safe enough he thought. He would turn out to be right as the IRS ignored his modest profits from his new holdings in these 3 companies.

Elizabeth had to be careful but would be so inclined to invest more in them too by giving a hint to Uncle Charlie, who required no more than a hint from those who had tipped him well in the past. John had enough money so wouldn't, but enjoyed the wit of it all, as he broke into a horse laugh worthy of the old Chairman, George Charles Lancer.

Elizabeth then said, "We are getting it done for Chuck. We have an agreement not to record or disclose his entering any of our correspondent bank locations or using any of their safe deposit boxes. He has the boxes under anonymous names, just by box number. Since the taxes have all been paid, that is no problem for us, him or the correspondent banks themselves. We have set up these boxes in correspondent banks so we are not involved and only he can audit the correctness of the bookkeeping. If all the money disappeared from all of them, I am sure he would let it go. As I said, he is easy to deal with."

"One more thing. We personally deliver the money to the boxes. We have already dispatched the carriers while on other rounds. They are given the key at the bank; return the key to another bonded individual there who mails it back to us. Very careful; and very smart I think. His idea of course."

John had always been a hunch player as Elizabeth had said earlier. He bet Canada. From the bio, Chuck had been a guide there. Chuck was rumored to have a little place up in Northern New England, a jumping off place to Canada. Chuck had been a guide in Algonquin Park. He would be smart enough not to go back there. But he had the skills. He would probably go deep to recover from years of hassling with Jack, to start with, and the police to end with.

It was a curious mystery. He thought he would give a stab at seeing Jim Johnstone, if at IBM now and if he were Jim Johnstone, or whoever impersonated him, which was more likely to be the case.

John used the occasion to think some more. Albert saw the signs and poured him a choice brandy. John was wondering why other entrepreneurs, and their families in particular, with an excess of cash who were into buybacks didn't stop hyping the stock and let it seek its natural level. That would make the stocks far cheaper to buy back. He was thinking in particular of the Walton family who were on their way to majority ownership of Walmart. Habit and ego he concluded. Well, Chuck didn't have the habit or the ego which made him smarter than the average bear, darn smart he concluded. This was a man to reckon with if anyone could find him.

No, he concluded, he was not necessarily in Canada. That's what a more traditional habit and ego person would do. He also wasn't necessarily not in Canada. A deep one, our boy, thought John, not for the first time. He would stay tuned if not necessarily tuning anyone else in. He had done his bit for the New York police and George. He would stand pat with his hand now, for himself, the Thatchers, and the Sloan.

Albert saw John had reached his conclusion. Becky did as well and silently slipped away as John and Albert sat together companionably with their 2 unfinished brandies.

Chapter 14

newport

There is only now, not yesterday or tomorrow

Chuck was happily ensconced in his place just north of Newport. He decided to wait at least a few more days before pushing off to his place across the lake in Magog, Quebec. From there he could take Route 10 into Montreal and go anywhere.

He had always thought the Banff National Park area would be good to live in so had bought a small place near there on about 20 acres of non-valuable but handsome property. He had quietly gone up a few months ago to stock it for this possible occasion. A few years before he had accepted a cash payment from an Italian company for everything.com services.

Pietro Romano had known Chuck some time and had asked about the possibility when Chuck was in Lake Como. Chuck asked how much he had in mind, "$7 Million USD and $3 million CDN."

Chuck liked the idea of cash from a foreign source, free from all encumbrances. It was not the tax he was trying to avoid; that was dangerous to do and silly with his wealth. No, it was the fact he could fund his separate identity when or if he needed it. After suitable negotiations, Chuck gave in. Chuck was willing to take the money at face value, but knew Pietro would find this unacceptable so thought of what else he could ask for.

Pietro had seen him thinking and let him do so. His investor would be delighted. The man was tainted, but not too much. Pietro liked to grant him favors. The man had approached Pietro in a roundabout way and asked if he could pay Romano the equivalent of $10 million US in US and Canadian cash and be repaid in a check in Euros.

The man was trusted because he always gave people who helped him something else, and equally important protected them from danger including himself. And this would be no exception, "Pietro, I helped you early and you appreciated it; I would appreciate this," the man had said.

That was enough, more than enough, for Pietro. "Certainly," Pietro had nodded respectfully. "It will be done."

"Pietro, you know I deeply appreciate your quick agreement. You have always left it to me to decide what I got for my investment, and other such things. You are doing it again. I appreciate it."

"You are welcome. You have been a wonderful supporter. Now tell me where this money is so I can figure out how to unload it with your approval. I must have your approval for my unloading. You must approve. If my first suggestion doesn't work, we will keep working at it until you like one."

"Wise of you as always, Pietro. $7 million is in US dollars and $3 million in Canadian dollars, both in the US; Canada is a smaller country but somehow we do better there. I hope that is OK."

At this stage the man was anxious so Pietro wanted to give him a quick solution. It didn't take him long to figure out Chuck would do it. And he told the man about Chuck. He did so at some length. The closing argument was, "Both my mistress and wife adore him. Isn't that something? My wife lets him stay over when I take my supposed business trips, which is in code, and she is fine with. They eat at the kitchen table. He speaks Italian. He likes it. He is the respectful son neither of us ever had," and the man laughed, always a good sign.

The man added, "You must be a second family to him?"

"No, not exactly, not precisely. He is like Daniel Boone or Robert Redford in <u>Jeremiah Johnson</u>. He can be with people but he is more comfortable by himself, a loner with others, but always a quiet handsome loner."

"In other words, Pietro, totally trustworthy."

"Yes, now that I think about it I would almost stake my life on it, but not quite," and they laughed together and the deal was done.

Then the man grew serious and said, "What can we give this Chuck in thanks? Certainly not more money I suspect."

"I think I know. We set up a Cayman Island account for his use with all the taxes properly paid for by us there. We let him use that to pay his bills in any way he wants. If he is who I think he is, he will want to go off on his own someday. His partner Jack is the frontman, but not one to be able to function without a Chuck. And the Chucks are rare as we know. Jack is jealous of him which is a terrible sign as you know; I met Jack; he is more like me in many ways, but not satisfied with today, always wanting more like a greedy child. No, that will come to bad ends. That's how we can help Chuck."

"How much from me, Pietro?"

"My friend, we have always done business simply. You decide that; you set up the account; you fund it."

"OK, but if we do more I will have to pay more."

"Only if you choose, only if you choose to do so. I have a test to verify for you what I believe; I will short change him a little; Chuck checks everything. He will know. But he will never say anything. If he says nothing then you know I am right; if not, then he is like the rest of us."

"I would be furious."

"Yes, you would, and I would. But that is why the Americans own the world. They fought the Italians didn't they? But immediately became our friends afterwards. They hold no grudges; they let things go. That is their secret sauce; they do not carry around wounds; they let them heal."

"Interesting man your Chuck."

"Yes, and I don't think he quite sees that but why should he? He is a man who truly lives in the present. You can see it when he eats or drinks; he enjoys just that, not what is next or what was before. Normally those people hang out in cafes and fail. He doesn't. But he is the only one of that type I know who has succeeded in business. Many succeed in life, according to their own analysis. It is odd."

"I see. If he splits from Jack, he will have to remove him, as we say in my business. Jack won't let him go quietly and might try to remove him first," and Pietro nodded.

The man continued, "So he will have use for this money. That is another reason to give it to him. It sounds as if he doesn't know he is in the removal business," and Pietro agreed, realizing he had learned a lot about Chuck's future, which in fact would come true, but he never shared his advance knowledge. The man would arrange the cash delivery as instructed by Pietro, set up the Cayman account, and that would be that.

Pietro informed Chuck; the US and Canadian money was delivered by arrangement in a U-Haul truck at an anonymous New York Thruway stop. Chuck had gotten the truck and drove it to his Newport house and buried it in a crypt he had built for that purpose in his woods. He counted the money and found the US money $25,000 short. Exactly $25,000 short. He wondered if that was a test; it surely was. Pietro was not careless and knew he was not. There must be someone else involved he correctly concluded. He would remain silent now and forevermore about the shortage.

89

He returned the U-Haul later the same day. The $3 million CDN was intact to the dollar. Interesting Chuck thought; the fine Italian hand, the fine Italian hand he thought. Out of his league for sure and he would leave it that way.

Pietro Romano was an immensely rich Italian who owned many things. His specialty was to create relationships early with emerging people and firms. He did this through LCs and now prepayments in the Internet days. He understood the Americans; they liked to be liked. Italians never understood that; Italians liked to be thought of as shrewd and sly, often outfoxing themselves.

The secret to dealing with Americans was to be simple, clear, fair, and pay on the dot. And they would overpay for that. No, Romano thought, no; their overpaying was a form of insurance. Who would you ship first? Who would you deal with first? The guy who paid you on the button or some Greek who would chisel you for sport? The Greeks were no fools; but they didn't understand what they valued put off others. Americans seeming naiveness was why they owned the world and certainly the cyberspace.

Pietro stayed active because his rich retired friends grew fat, lazy, stupid, and worst of all boring. He did not want to go down that road. A secret of Pietro's is he knew he, too, was vulnerable to all human vices and had to remain vigilant to control them the best he could.

Romano liked Chuck because he let Pietro be himself. He never begrudged him his negotiations, rantings, objections, carryings on, mistresses, and more.

In fact, his most passionate mistress always asked when Chuck was coming over next. She had been useful as well as gorgeous as well as rich and care free due to Romano's generosity, what Chuck would call his basic fairness. But even Chuck did not have the nerve to call, no accuse, Romano of being fair. Pietro would have been offended at such candor and praise, and this from a man who seemed candid.

When the 3 of them went out together the first time Chuck treated Pietro's mistress like the lady she wanted to be but could not afford to be since the mistressing job paid better and gave a woman more freedom in Italy. She loved the way he spoke literate Italian that she was sure Dante himself would have admired. And the payoff for Romano was she was incredibly passionate and wonderful for the rest of their weekend together.

Romano's wife liked Chuck because she knew Pietro would be safe with him. As with many Italian wives, she had sex for children not for sport. She left the sport to Pietro and his mistresses who worked far harder at that than she ever had as a wife or mother.

As a result, Chuck was one of the few business associates of Pietro that she warmly invited into her house, as she thought of it, and made a house guest. When Pietro would leave for a business weekend, thinly veiled for one with a mistress, Chuck would stay over if in town and they would eat quietly at her kitchen table. The house was elegant as befitting an Italian Robber Baron as she thought of her husband. But she preferred the kitchen as did Chuck.

Romano knew why his mistresses and wife both liked Chuck. He was some kind of female dream. He was handsome, if not gorgeous, respectful, and not pushy. He had a knack of letting others do the approaching. Above all he let people be themselves and enjoyed letting them be so. The man could have been Daniel Boone, he always thought. A true American loner, though Boone was more in image than in reality he had learned when reading more about him.

Chuck knew the Italians liked to negotiate, in fact hated it when one didn't. Although Jack had the charisma, the Mediterranean

91

customers preferred Chuck because he was capable of enduring cumbersome negotiations and Jack was not.

Chuck had created a separate identity complete with US passport and photos, and all that goes with it. It cost him a handsome sum but it did handsome work. He had been working on the profile for some time. He chose the name John Miller because there were lots of them. It had worked to date. He now had credit cards, library cards, and more. He had also created an almost brother, Jim Miller, who had the same set of documents but for Canada, which he occasionally used as well.

Since many things in Canada were free that cost money elsewhere, they were more complicated. So Chuck had started a little Canadian company, paid Jim Miller as an employee to get his Canadian equivalent of social security going, his national health card, and more. He had also bought a nice condo in Vancouver as another place to go when the weather got tough in Banff, which it did in the winter in the Canadian Rockies.

Chuck knew that people thought it was safe to go deep in the wilderness but he knew better. Any outpost got to know you fast because so few people passed through and seeing a new person was an uplifting thing, not the nuisance it was for most storekeepers in town.

He had his plan. First Newport. Then Magog. Then on to Banff by train. Then on to Vancouver by train. And on to Honolulu by ship. He could run the businesses from wherever. Janet Brown indicated she would stay with the business. So she could run Simply. The other division would be tucked under Simply and he could let her run both.

No he paused in thought as he walked quietly around his property. He was the fox and they were the hounds. They didn't know where his lair was. The last thing he should be doing is moving. Deer froze in place. The human eye saw what moved. It was time not to move. And what did that entail he wondered?

He had 6 months of supplies stocked away in Newport. He had 2 weeks of fresh things. He would forgo the fresh and stay in his lair for 6 months. As he had learned in preparation for his new adventure as he thought of it, statistically the police either got their perpetrator quickly or not at all usually. In his case, though, they would figure out it could only be him as the candidate, the logical candidate, which he added to by leaving and ratified further by being unavailable so their odds of capture had to be better than average in his case.

He had learned through Internet backdoor ways there was no warrant or subpoena out for him. They were looking but had no justifiable cause to get formal court sanctioning for doing so. Good for him. Each day that passed would be a good one; each day that passed would put other cases in front of his.

He had bought a section of land around his Newport place under different names, using a Wyoming savings bank to pay for them. Nail that stick up get hammered hard, he thought, not for the first time. Multiple owners purchasing at different times did not cause the town clerk to gossip about a rich property owning flatlander in town. And if so, then it would be a Wyoming guy, not a Northeast flatlander.

Under the Wyoming identity he had hired some wilderness landscape people to craft and clear out subtle trails that were fun to walk. 640 acres provided lots of walking room. He couldn't really buy more even with surrogates or it would stand out as too much open space to go unnoticed, especially with new mapping tech.

As he walked further, he realized that he needed to simplify the business not complicate it. He had enough cash and equivalents out of the business to last him 10 or more lifetimes as a spendthrift and forever with his personality and predilections.

He had invested $10 million in each Walmart, Dollar Tree, Apple, and Amazon. Walmart dividends had started out at about 2% of market value or $200,000 per year; Apple, Dollar

Tree, and Amazon had not yet started paying dividends but the stocks had increased multiple times since his purchase. He thought Apple would start paying dividends soon. Walmart, Dollar Tree, and Apple also had stock repurchase programs in place to put a floor under the stock by having fewer shares to pay dividends on if they paid them or later if they decided to pay them. And, of course as he knew, by buying their own stock, which they knew, they didn't buy something new that they did not know and distract themselves as Jack so often had.

So to trim his sails he decided on his walk, as he looked at the beautiful Rousseau like Swiss vista of Northern Vermont, he would consolidate his large division under the Simply umbrella. He would not ask Janet Brown to run it. He would let her stay retired as she had said she wanted to, for negotiation purposes he suspected, and he was right about that.

Simply was a simple sustainable business with no cost of goods for current titles; about 150 had author splits, but only after money was received. He could judiciously buy out most if not all of those authors which would further simplify and privatize matters. Over time that was done.

As for the other niche lines, they emphasized basic products in apparel, sports, shoes, hardware, and home goods. They competed with Amazon which was not good, but generally had better prices than they did since they focused on the lower price part of the market not the higher end where most cyber companies were and wanted to be, including Amazon itself.

Yes, that was it. He would start tomorrow. As he smiled while walking, he reminded himself all he had was now, not yesterday or tomorrow. And that would be true as it always is though most people were unmindful of that simple truth, he mused.

Chapter 15

Lunch

Patience and time are the ultimate warriors

George and Joyce were looking forward to their second meeting, drinks, and dinner. It was a lovely break from everything else in their lives. They had taken the day off, kind of a Sunday as they thought of it, with a nice party at the end to top it off.

Albert loved entertaining; Elizabeth and John were thoughtful. They had discussed it earlier and came to no firm conclusions but some suggestive ones.

Elizabeth came over to lunch with Albert and her father. They all enjoyed getting lunches started together; they worked amiably together in the kitchen getting a salad done; and fish to justify the night's upcoming steak and potatoes extravaganza Albert and John liked so much.

When they sat down, Elizabeth said, "Dad, I have been following everything.com since yesterday. Things are going smoothly there. Things are smoother than before of course since the unprofitable division has been pawned off on IBM who was desperate for top line growth."

"Yes," thought John. "Being private means you can concentrate on the money. IBM can't do that. Becky, since we are Dad, Becky, and Albert now, give us the run down as of right now."

"As you know, increasing positive cash flow tends to be more positive and negative cash flow more negative than planned. This situation at Simply and everything.com is no exception. Let me give you the details," as she paused to have a bite of the orange and strawberry salad they had all just made.

"This morning we were notified that all the sites would now come in the marketplace through the Simply umbrella, saving the complexity of multiple site payments. The consumer will see all of the sites separately; but the back office will be cleaner, crisper, simpler, and therefore cheaper."

"A revised corporate masthead shows only Chuck as an officer and the Sloan as agent. As you know that is perfectly legal; but we thought Janet Brown might be included and she wasn't. That probably means no new staff. In any event, when we got ready to setup the first week's payroll we learned there would be no employees so no payroll."

"No employees in a $900 million business? Isn't that risky?" John said.

"Not if there are no employees, Dad. Now here is the second part of it. When queried about office rents, warehouses, and such things, which the presale company had, we were told that IBM owned and controlled them all now, not everything.com."

"So, Becky, is he planning to run this out of his back pocket?"

"It would appear so, yes."

With that John signaled Albert who got him a tall scotch to get through this. Albert had one too and looked at Becky, who didn't wave him off. So they sat there companionably sipping their scotches for a few minutes.

They waited for John to speak and he did: "I take back my hunch he is in Canada. I'll bet he has prepared a hidey hole in the US and has dug deeply into it. Smart. Moving feels right, as animals do, like squirrels that run in front of your car. But the risks are higher."

"No, I'd bet he is still here, probably in Northern New England where he would feel comfortable. People in New England forget the latitude in Northern New England is similar to

96

Algonquin Park, north of Toronto since southern Ontario dips down substantially versus New England. As a Park guide he would feel comfortable in the familiar landscape of Northern New England."

"And Becky, I don't think the Sloan should help further to find him because you may well have him be willing to do a make good for our investors."

"Yes, I can see that. He might give up some money to our investors who got hurt on the dip that he benefited from. By my analysis as I said before, our people lost $1 billion at the $20 billion valuation. At $10 billion $500 million, I think he would be amenable to that since that is what our agreements with the investors said they had to sell at. That should work."

"Really," said Albert. "Some guy."

"Yes, Albert, some guy. You got it exactly right. I don't think he had any interest in taking our people down. Even our funds. He had and has worked with us and was loyal to us. Is for that matter; so we can reciprocate."

John said, "Becky, how do we do this? I think I see where you are going. Let me try," as she nodded. "$500 million though a ton of money to most is less than a year's profit and cashflow to him," as she nodded. "Solidifying the deal with us would certainly be worth it to him." She nodded again as he went on, "And now I think I am on the right track here, he isn't really such a money oriented guy. I am seeing this."

"In fact he reminds me of one of our entrepreneurial successes who said to me once in confidence, as if he were giving up a deep dark trade secret, 'John, it sounds wimpy to say but after a certain amount of money it is only a question of how much more one gives to charity.'"

"Yes, that seems to be him except he isn't a charity type guy. He is a loner, a guide. He doesn't want to go to black tie parties to impress people; he has no wife to push him to do so, which is the more common reason billionaires do that."

"Also, you have shown a new light upon the man," as her eyebrows went up. "Yes, he realized that he couldn't escape Jack other than to kill him. I'll bet he tried many ways to escape short of that and failed," she nodded twice at that. "Yes, I see that. Jack was getting increasingly imperial as those types do; as we know, the Napoleonic tendency was not limited to Napoleon. Chuck was undoubtedly cornered into killing his partner, and he did do it in the gentlest way possible."

"Self-defense, in fact; not technically, but that is what it amounted to," John concluded. Once again Elizabeth and Albert were stunned about the way John cut through the fog to the heart of the matter.

Elizabeth, and that was how she was thinking of herself now, not Becky, remembered John's classic quotation from Dr. Johnson, "Nothing is quite as innocent as a person seeking money." They aren't perfect doing so but the motives were better than others, which was a stunner to her at the time and had proven to be right to her over and over again since then.

Chuck just wanted enough of it. Jack wanted so much more like Alexander the Great. Jack was the dangerous one as Dr. Johnson had noted in the 17th Century. Jack cornered Chuck and would have edged him out and possibly have him killed as Alexander the Great put 100,000s to the sword as a matter of routine when taking over a town that opposed him initially by requiring a siege to seize it which he would have done to Chuck for resisting him.

Elizabeth interjected, "One thing is clear. The police won't see it our way. So what do we do in a few hours?"

"Nothing is best," Albert said.

Elizabeth continued, "Yes, Albert, nothing is best. But I don't think we will get away with nothing. If we try, the shift will be too dramatic. George is too smart and Joyce will pick up on it too. No, we must be helpful."

John then said, "But from behind, not leading the charge. We do have a fiduciary duty on our side, especially if Chuck agrees to Elizabeth's $500 million proposal. I think Elizabeth, if you can see your way to it, you should email the offer now. If you get agreement from Chuck, we know what to do. I assume he is quick with you, knowing you like that as he evidently does too," and she nodded.

"OK. That's the plan," John Putnam Thatcher concluded as Chairman of the Board.

It felt like they were synchronizing their watches, which, in a way,   they   were.

Chapter 16

Thatcher II

Every day I try to figure out what is going on

The Thatchers and Albert were dreading the dinner George and Joyce were looking forward to so much. At a minimum they would have to dissemble, and it would get worse from there.

As Elizabeth had thought, Chuck's email agreed to her proposal. He suggested the Sloan find a way to skim off, as he put it, the $500 million in such a way as not to raise red flags to any outsiders such as the tax authorities but to be sure it was tax correct and in no way tax avoidance.

So cautious; exactly like Chuck and why she liked working with him. It was always better to have a client more cautious than you so you could nudge them along towards risk versus having to always restrain them, and fearing one day you might fail and disaster would ensue, as it so often did with those types who pushed the envelope.

Elizabeth was pleased. She agreed, sent Chuck a confirmation email, and said she would work out the details. Chuck wrote back, evidently because it was not a personalized email, that this should serve as his authorization to do so and he would follow events as they unfolded.

She told John and Albert. They were more pleased than they expected to be and said so. John went on, "Elizabeth, Good of you to solve this one."

She had figured out how to handle it. She would let the shareholders know she had recaptured their money in a private settlement after she got the money, with the primary provision is it be kept secret.

She would pass this along to Everett, VP of No, who would surely approve of any financial repatriation for any sin. That could wait until the smoke cleared a bit more.

She asked John about this, "Yes, Elizabeth. You have the agreement; why not start taking the money and put it in a sinking fund. That is totally reasonable. Then you can decide in 30 days what you want to do next including staying quiet about it. Less said, soonest mended, etc. and so on."

Albert nodded. They had their plan and now would wait a few hours for Joyce and George. John suggested they take a walk; they did so. It did them good. They got back about 4:30 PM and waited for their timely guests who were primarily on business but with a social side to it.

When they arrived, some congenial drinking began. George had decided to wait until John or Elizabeth brought up the subject before leaving the social for the business. He would have a long wait because Albert called them to the table for dinner without the business being raised.

This forced George's hand because, as he started to realize, the Thatchers were waiting him out. He suspected they could wait right through dinner, after dinner drinks, and goodbye.

So George launched in, "Well, what did you learn?"

"Nothing really," John said, taking a sip of his Scotch to bolster his flagging spirits having to dissemble with George who he liked and Joyce who he had come to like as well.

George thought that sounded like a Jim Johnson answer. He followed up with, "Did you learn anything?"

"In the negative, yes. There is no Jim Johnson reported at IBM now or in the former everything.com company. So it seems he was entirely fictitious," John said. He had phoned IBM; this was true; but it was a total distraction, dissembling at his best he thought. Or at least the best he could do.

George interjected, "Yes, we learned that too. I am sure you were apt to get a warmer reception than we did," George added.

"Not really. We represent New York and we might as well be the police in their minds, which is understandable from their perspective," John added to fill up the conversational space as the main course was finishing, Albert and Elizabeth had stood up, and they cleared the table. John had given Albert the high sign to have no dessert and John led the way to the living room for after dinner drinks.

John had put out the brandy as a signal. George picked up the signal but had a brandy anyway though it moved things along faster than he otherwise would have liked; but he knew the brandy would be magnificent and was. The differences in wines or beers were no big deal in his mind; but ah, brandy. He enjoyed his brandy quietly for a few minutes and let the silence embrace and mellow them, which it did with brandy at hand and a wonderful dinner eaten.

In short it felt a bit like a prisoner's last supper, George thought. Well, if so, it was a darn good one, he would give the Thatchers and Albert that.

"John, you don't seem as talkative as last night."

"Probably my New Hampshire roots. When I have nothing to say I try to say nothing. I guess the real story is the trail is getting cold; we didn't pick up anything at the bank," as Elizabeth nodded. "We didn't pick up anything in Tucson. So where else would we look? What do you think? What would you like us to do?"

John had him cornered. George didn't know either. He thought it prudent to say that and did. There was a pause. Joyce stepped into it, "Well, we will let you know how we are doing and ask

102

you to do what you can when we know more. We will leave you to it as they say," and got up to leave.

George noticed that Albert was instantly on his feet trying to be helpful as John and Elizabeth held their ground, slowly standing up to say their goodbyes, trying to curb their enthusiasm rather successfully he thought.

When they were out and on the street George said, "That was the bums' rush."

Joyce said, "Yes, the uptown bums' rush. I thought it best to leave to fight another day."

George grimaced and said, "Will we have another day with them? Will we? I smelled Jim Johnson in there."

Joyce was almost crushed by the comment. As she started to recover she said, "Was I wrong?"

"Yes, my dear, you were. You let the hospitality absorb you. I was wrong too because I was your partner in crime on that one. Thatcher is a deep one; he always has been; hand it to him. We will have to think about it. But it was the bums' rush and I don't know if we will get back in again, ever." He would be right.

Chapter 17

Commissioner

Less is more in most things

The Commissioner had called a second meeting to update him. While not necessarily a good thing, his meetings got you noticed. Every previous meeting had led to something good for George, large or small. The meetings themselves were fairly grim though. He expected this one would be as well.

He thought about warning Joyce about this but realized she was more of the Commissioner's class than he was so was probably better suited to it than he. And she was better looking; and the Commissioner did notice such things.

At 10 AM the next day the meeting commenced. They were again led into a large corner office, more familiar to large investment firms than police stations. The regal secretary was regal again to make the point that they were going into anointed chambers. George had always found the reminder helpful; not everyone did.

With no amenities they just sat down. The Commissioner had several assistants in the room including a stenographer, intimidating in and of itself. He only did that when politics were involved, when he was less interested in the facts than the appearance of them. George took the point and prepared himself to give the kinds of answers appropriate to that circumstance.

"Well Parsons. Give us your report," the Commissioner was in his regal last name, "we", and "us" mode not the "I" and "me" one which he was equally skilled at. He had made his point and looked sharply at George to be sure he took it. Being satisfied with that, he nodded and George began.

George recounted the story, largely full of negatives of course. He was candid, clear, and crisp in his answers. The Commissioner was always a good guide. If he did not like the way a political discussion was going, he would make a nonverbal gesture; he had not done that so George believed he was on the right track or at least not on the wrong one. He was right about that.

At the end of the story the Commissioner asked a simple yet crisp question, "What now George?"

"I am not sure. What would you suggest, sir?"

The Commissioner clearly did not like being put on the spot; but being a fair man, which he was, he understood it was not an unreasonable question. What should he say was written on his face. He paused and said truthfully, "I am not sure. What are your thoughts and those of Officer Allison?"

Joyce answered this time: "We discussed exactly that before your first meeting with us and again last night with the Thatchers. I think we must wait on this one. No one involved seems to be left in New York; all of the party goers were hired by IBM and moved virtually instantly to Arizona."

"The old office was let go and another firm, BOA, now occupies it. The owner condos similarly were sold and let go; now a reclusive hedge fund guy owns and occupies both. Quite simply, nothing and nobody is left in our jurisdiction. So what do we do about that? That is the question, sir."

George left Joyce's question on the table without comment. He truly did not know either and thought it best to throw the mess on the table for all to see. The Commissioner saw that; all he could think of is that he shouldn't have called this meeting in the first place. He had been cornered in his own office.

105

The hot potato had been thrown back to him. Being an honest man he admitted to himself that this was only fair. So there it was. They sat there for a minute looking at each other. The good thing about transcripts is they only recorded words, not silences like the moment they were having.

It became clear to the Commissioner that they were waiting for him. They would not be provoked into an answer. Wise of them he thought; not that he found that idea comforting or helpful. It was what it was and they had helped him reach that point. He believed they had opened the bag, with nothing left in it to chew on. At least for now. He was appreciative of their clarity as he always was with George and believed he would be of Joyce now and in the future. He would be right about that.

So he answered, back on a more cordial first name basis, "Thank you George and Joyce. We will get back to you," and that was that as the meeting ended.

George complimented Joyce on the way out. "We did that well; we held our ground. We did not advance or retreat. Good work, Joyce."

"Thank you, George. The Commissioner was fair about it wasn't he? He handled it well, don't you think?"

"Yes. Best Commissioner we have ever had. Does his job properly; doesn't blame the underlings. He took our measure and that of the situation. That in and of itself was helpful. I have never known him to give suggestions, instructions, or a next meeting date just to hear himself talk, as so many political appointees do. That was a message in and of itself. In short, he, too, knows we have to wait out events with every witness now out of our jurisdiction."

And that was that as they went their separate ways home.

Chapter 18

Back Story

Most answers are in history

Some things come to a quick conclusion, others a slow one, and a few drag on. Unsolved murders drag on because there is no statute of limitations on them. A cold case is forever capable of being activated. But there needs to be new proof to activate it. And none of the parties that might provide proof, or pointers to the proof, were in the New York City jurisdiction now nor were likely to be anytime soon, which was no small thing. This was a local not state or federal crime. Other cities and states had their own issues; this was not one of them.

Chuck stayed deep. After some thought he had decided that a first step was to make good on the Sloan investors as Elizabeth suggested. The quid pro quo subtlely stated was the Sloan and their talent would then leave him alone. That was definitely a big factor in his decision, though not the only one. He had meant no harm to those investors and thought it fair they be compensated for Chuck's untimely death and resulting hit on the stock price.

Chuck would stay deep until they were repaid the $500 million. He calculated that would take about 300 days; he would mark them off on his calendar as the money was repaid because he liked counting. In fact he chuckled; he lived by counting, whether it was numbers, calories, books he owned or anything else. It was a fetish he knew, but not a harmful one he thought.

So with regard to the Sloan, each day that passed reflected a reduction in his obligation of a third of 1%, 3 days would be 1%, and so on and so on until the obligation was retired. He appreciated that Elizabeth would handle matters on the Sloan end without involving him further. She was expert at this and he was not.

As he contemplated this last part of discharging the old company problems, he recognized that he liked everything that was available on his Newport property. He had a lake, hiking trails, wilderness without scary animals that might eat you, no poisonous snakes and such, and the 4 seasons to enjoy and complain about as New Englanders enjoyed doing. He never did; but he also always enjoyed the moment: the promise of spring; the hot days of summer; the colors of fall; and the clarity of winter. All good, each in their own way as most things were he thought. Well, he was getting contemplative, wasn't he, he thought. Yes, but now was the time for it after a lifetime of straight ahead work. Ah, he said; I'll have to get used to this.

Chuck enjoyed the thought of the consolidation of everything under the Simply umbrella. The basic growth of the industry, coupled with Simply's opening price point cheap high quality product offerings, fit the times. The business was growing nicely as were the profits. He thought his 3 goals for the next 300 days should be to pay off the $500 million, streamline the company, and enjoy himself without moving off his property except for getting required supplies. In fact, he thought; he should be able to push the 6 months to 10 months, which would do it to never leave at all, much as Thoreau had said in *Walking* about Concord. No need to go anywhere else; well there was that wasn't there, he considered.

A year before he had added his 1000th book to his Newport library. He had replaced the former house with an elegant cabin with modern conveniences and just a few large rooms to keep the cabin feeling. He did not want a house.

The cabin foot print was just 900 feet. He had 2 floors. The cabin was sited facing south on a slight rise overlooking a stream, field, lake, and pleasant low Vermont mountains. The living room and library extended the length of the cabin and half way across. The brick floored kitchen was next to it for about a third of the that half of the space. Behind it on that side was a bedroom, shower and toilet for easy access to clean up from traipsing around outside when coming off the screened in porch into the kitchen.

The windows were boxed colonial style as in Williamsburg to give a cozy feeling versus brazen picture windows. A Vermont Castings stove in the kitchen gave off a warmth, heat, and pleasure. A stone porch extended off the living room and library with steps down to the ground and just a few more paces to the cow path he created down to the stream, across it to his field and lake, with the low mountains in the background.

The upstairs consisted of his bedroom and study extending the length of the house too, directly above the living room and library, and a second one doing the same on the other side over the kitchen and downstairs bedroom, with a full bathroom between. He had an attic and basement but had little use for them being single with no wife or family to fill it up with their unused things. He kept the rooms spare because cabins were that way and stuff just got in the way in his mind.

The cabin had a septic system, backup generator that could run for weeks if required, and a sophisticated surveillance system. He had marked off his section of land with a serious, if carefully disguised, high metal fence and well hidden moat nearer the cabin. His single narrow road in had a high locked gate. He had video surveillance cameras around the property activated by motion, which usually was done by animals but occasionally by a trespasser.

He had had 2 in the time he had owned the property. The first seemed challenged by the fence; climbed it; wandered around a bit; looked in a surveillance camera; thought better of being there and left.

Just 15 days ago the second expert climbed the fence and fell into the moat he camouflaged nearer the house. The intruder had a serious rifle and military camouflage gear on, so was clearly up to no good. He never got out of the moat. Chuck thought that was just as well.

Chuck was a mountain man so tracked the man's trail back to a car with a Wyoming license plate parked some 3 miles away. He investigated. In his car was evidence Jack had hired this killer to take him out.

Chuck knew he could not leave things as they were. He had to roll up this guy's life so no one would come looking for him or check out his property. The secrecy the man had to employ not to be arrested helped Chuck cover his own tracks as well. If you live by the sword you die by the sword, Chuck thought not for the first time.

The man's ID was in the car. He had his computer and communication devices with him and lived alone in a rented place outside of Sheridan, Wyoming. Chuck then went back to the moat, killed the intruder with a couple of shots, stripped the body, and hauled him out to his car which was some effort since Chuck had to carry him 3 miles through deep woods and this was a big man.

Then, he emailed the owner of the guy's place; canceled his lease; told the owner to keep the deposit; sell his stuff off since he was in Florida. An hour later the landlord confirmed and wished him well. He said he had a renter lined up anyway so not to worry about it. Chuck sensed from the email the owner was afraid of the killer, certainly with good reason, and was pleased he was moving on. Good.

Chuck had then driven the car back to his place; incinerated the body; dumped the ashes in the stream; and driven the car back to Boston. At about 7 AM, after removing the license plates, Chuck left the car with the keys in it near a chop shop in the old Irish section of South Boston. He checked back at 10 AM and the car was gone.

110

He took the bus from South Station to Littleton, New Hampshire, and found a high school kid to drive him up to Newport, where he walked the last 3 miles into his property. Being in no hurry helped with his doing this anonymously by taking the low end bus and then waiting for a kid to leave McD's where he was working to pay him for a ride to drive him up north. He paid well but not too well, to avoid being talked about.

This was the why of it about his killing Jack. But Chuck knew that any disclosure of the why of it to any authorities would lead to 2 murder charges, albeit with some self-defense justification. But a good DA would defeat him on reasonable force in the first instance and certainly in the second. Mitigation might lead to a sentence of no more than 20 years, but that was a huge risk and a long time inside. So Chuck decided to live with the risk, but with a clear conscience, at least in his own mind.

Jack had been somewhat surprised to see Chuck a few days later, just before the Simply announcement. It took an experienced person to see Jack's consternation upon seeing him. Chuck knew he had to take Jack out in a few days or risk another attempt on his life. He delivered on that with the party poisoning.

Jack jarred himself loose from those old thoughts and focused on everything.com and Simply customers who were happy with the fast service, focused offerings, and cheap price points. He viewed the business like throwing a pebble into a lake; the ripples spread out as long as one didn't disturb the rest of the lake, which he didn't plan to do.

He instructed himself not to get caught up in ever hyping the business because there was no need to do so since there were no employees to pay, stock options to grow, or investors to satisfy. He was the entire audience, well at least after the Sloan had their $500 million he would be.

When the $500 million was repaid Chuck would have a drink of Costco bourbon, a fine bourbon indeed, meeting his dual personal standards of quality and cheapness, an unbeatable duo.

Just as that Sloan obligation was completely repaid about 300 days later, Romano wrote him to see if he would take a luxury house, car, and furniture in Key Biscayne in return for $3 million USD. Pietro added that they would deliver the home ownership as he desired or through the trust in the Caymans. Chuck agreed and was told to get a similar U-Haul at the New York Thruway stop he had picked up the $7 million USD and $3 million CDN before. Chuck followed the instructions again.

Pietro was most pleased and said he would add something else to the pot. Boat, wine, women, what?

Chuck wrote back that a boat and wine would be nice but not to be unreasonably generous. He wanted to remain liked. Pietro liked his wit and humility, a rare combination; Pietro wrote back saying his lady friend and wife were looking forward to seeing him soon.

Then Pietro wrote back a few days later that Chuck had to come over soon because of pressure on the home front to have him as a dining and house guest again. He had arranged for Chuck to come over on a luxury cruise in which he could remain anonymous getting on and off, which he knew Chuck liked. Chuck agreed. He would use his John Miller papers, as required, with his own as backup.

So on the right date Chuck got the McD kid to give him a ride from outside Newport to Littleton, took the bus from there to South Station, and Amtrak down to Ft. Lauderdale; got on the cruise, and stayed in Italy for six months. He saw no reason to come back for a while so wandered around Europe perfecting his French, Italian, Spanish, and Greek. He owned the house on Key Biscayne but had not seen it yet.

After 5 years or so floating around Europe, Pietro got him back anonymously again and he saw the lovely property on Key Biscayne, staying there a few years before Amtraking back anonymously again North to South Station.

Chuck's life played out like that. Simply grew nicely, threw off a lot of cash with which Chuck really had no use for so it just piled up, remained personally quiet and under radar. Chuck enjoyed it. He called it BigCo now, which it was now for sure.

One night the latest of Pietro's mistresses had asked Chuck what he did for women. He told her honestly; "I seek women who are between things; when they find what they want I give them a bon voyage present of some value. They like that."

"Yes," she said, "they would, especially when they get to choose."

"Well," Chuck said, "One way or another women always do. If they are happy, you are happy; if not, you will be unhappy with them. So why not just move on down the road?"

The 3 of them drank to that. And Chuck continued to live his life   like   that.

Chapter 19

Epilogue

Is it the end of a story or the beginning of another

George eventually retired. He never let the case go. But he never got further with it either. The case was a burr under his saddle; but that was life, he figured.

Joyce went on to big things. She became Police Commissioner and then Senator. She never made President.

More's the pity thought many who knew her. She would have outclassed them all. But you had to know her for that knowledge. She was a grand Senator in the Henry Clay and John Calhoun tradition. Good enough, but not quite enough to become president.

The Thatchers and Albert remained themselves. The Sloan was the Sloan, prospering in Dublin and as a private company.

Chuck kept a tight rein on the business so he could float through the world as the canoe guide he had been and still was in his own mind. He was like a stone, pretty happy where ever he was dropped.

John Putnam Thatcher had the last word on Jack at a dinner with Elizabeth and Albert. "I went to visit his gravestone. I had a hunch that something would be written on it, I am not sure why I thought that. There was and in *Spoon River* style it said:

I lie here troubled because no one came to my funeral

They nodded as John concluded, "And we know who the executor was."

The End

Made in the USA
Lexington, KY
08 June 2019